Shotgun
Saturday Night

Also by Bill Crider
Too Late to Die

Shotgun Saturday Night

A Sheriff Dan Rhodes Mystery

Bill Crider

Walker and Company
New York

First published in the United States of America in 1987 by the
Walker Publishing Company, Inc.

Published simultaneously in Canada by
Thomas Allen & Son
Canada, Limited, Markham, Ontario

Library of Congress Cataloging-in-Publication Data

Crider, Bill, 1941–
    Shotgun Saturday night.

    I. Title.
PS3553.R497S5 1987   813'.54   87-13354
ISBN 0-8027-5684-0

Printed in the United States of America

10 9 8 7 6 5 4 3 2 1

To All the Members of DAPA-EM—
Past and Present

1

SHERIFF DAN RHODES knew it was going to be a bad day when Bert Ramsey brought in the arm and laid it on the desk.

The arm was neatly wrapped in a sheet of clear plastic, which was circled in three places with plastic strapping tape, the kind with fibers running through it. The arm was pale and bloodless and had been cleanly severed from the torso at the shoulder.

"Got another one out in the truck," Bert said around the wad of snuff he had tucked between his cheek and gum on the left side of his mouth. "Got a couple of legs, too, but they don't match up with each other."

Bert Ramsey was a short, wiry man with a sun- and windburned face. Rhodes had once seen a briefcase made of industrial belting leather. Ramsey's face looked as if it were made of the same material.

Hack Jensen got up from his broken-down swivel chair by the radio and walked over to Rhodes's desk. He was a tall, thin old man, who had always reminded Rhodes of the comedian Bud Abbott, though he certainly didn't sound like him.

"Good Lord," Hack said. "Where'd you find that thing?"

Ramsey reached out and touched the arm, making the plastic crackle. "Down to the old Caster place," he said. "I been clearing brush down there."

Bert did odd jobs all over Blacklin County, preferring to work outside and with his hands. He strung and stretched barbed wire, roofed houses, built sheds, baled hay, painted, cleared brush, and generally did whatever came to hand.

Rhodes sighed and leaned back in his chair, causing the spring underneath it to make a high-pitched squeal. "Who owns the Caster place now?" he asked.

Hack answered. "Some folks named Adams. Bought it a couple years ago."

"That's right," Ramsey said. "They live down in Houston. Called me last weekend to ask about me clearing the brush."

Rhodes slid his chair back and stood up. "I guess we better have a look in your truck and then go on out there," he said. He walked over to a scarred hat rack that had been there since long before he had taken office and took down his hat.

"You want me to let Buddy or the new deputy know about this?" Hack asked.

"No," Rhodes said. "Not yet. Let's go, Bert."

Outside, the late-August sun and the scorching westerly breeze were enough to take your breath away. As the two men walked down past the low wrought-iron fence that surrounded the jail, Rhodes looked back wistfully at the back of the window-unit air conditioner hanging from the side of the jail. Condensation from its coils was dripping down into the red dirt, turning it to mud.

Bert Ramsey's pickup was parked in front of the walk. It was a blue Chevy S-10, and in the back Rhodes could see three more of the plastic packages, all neatly wrapped, the ends turned carefully down and bound with the strapping tape. There was another arm and the two legs Ramsey had mentioned. One of the legs was short; the other was quite a bit longer.

Rhodes laid his left hand on the hot side of the pickup

and pushed his hat back slightly with his right. "I wouldn't believe this if I weren't seeing it," he said.

"Me either," Ramsey said. "And that ain't all."

"There's more?"

Ramsey nodded.

"Let's have the whole thing," Rhodes said.

"Well," Ramsey said, "I went down to the Caster place this mornin' to burn some brush. I been clearin' down there since Monday. Lots o' brush stacked up here and there." He paused.

"I can imagine," Rhodes said. There wasn't a cloud in the sky, and he could feel the sweat beginning to trickle down his ribs.

"Yeah," Ramsey said. "Anyways, I went down there, and all up in one of the brush piles was these boxes."

"What kind of boxes?"

"Just boxes. Cardboard boxes. Good, solid cardboard, though. Corrugated. All wrapped up with brown plastic tape, tight as drums. I naturally wondered what was in 'em, seeing as how I didn't put 'em there. They sure as heck weren't there when I left yesterday afternoon, late. So I opened one of 'em up."

"And this is what you found?"

"Yep. Scared hell out of me, I can tell you that. A whole box full of arms and legs, just comin' out of nowhere, almost. I don't usually scare easy, but that set me back some. I figured I better bring 'em in to you."

"You said 'boxes.' You mean there's more than one?"

"Two more I didn't open," Ramsey said. "I figured if it was arms and legs in the first one, I didn't even want to see in the others."

Rhodes didn't particularly want to see, either. He'd never dealt with mass killing before, never even considered the possibility of it. Not in a place like Blacklin County. "I guess I better go on down there and check it out," he said. "You go in the truck. I'll follow you in the county car."

Rhodes turned away, but Ramsey called him back. "What about these?" Ramsey asked, gesturing toward the back of his S-10.

"We'll just have to take them with us," Rhodes said. "I guess a few more hours in the sun won't hurt them." He remembered the arm that was still in his office. He hoped that Hack would have sense enough to get it out of sight, just in case anyone happened to come by. "After we check out the other two boxes, well, we'll just have to see."

"I guess so," Ramsey said, not looking any too happy about it. He got in his pickup, and Rhodes walked around to the side of the jail to get the county car. He was looking forward to turning on the air conditioner, but as soon as he did, a blast of hot air hit him in the face. It would take a while for the air to get cool enough to help.

The Caster place was about nine miles from Clearview, the county seat of Blacklin County. The road was straight and narrow, with deep ditches on either side. Rhodes had heard that it was built in an old railroad bed, which was probably true. As he followed the little blue pickup, Rhodes thought about the body parts in the boxes. He could hardly believe that something like that could turn up in an out-of-the-way place like this, but on second thought he decided that no one would try to dispose of arms and legs in a public park in Houston, either. Or maybe they would.

In fact, the more he thought about it, the more logical it seemed. The road he was driving on was a farm-to-market road that was actually only a few miles from an interstate highway, and connected to the highway by another farm-to-market road. Someone looking to get rid of a body or two might easily come off the interstate,

4

look for a wooded area, spot the brush piles, and leave the boxes and their grisly contents there. If whoever had dumped the boxes had been lucky, Bert Ramsey might have burned them without ever looking inside.

The thought that the boxes might have come over from the interstate made Rhodes feel a little better. He couldn't think of anyone missing in Blacklin County, much less three or four people. At least, people weren't disappearing right under his nose.

The blinker on Bert's pickup began flashing for a right turn, and Rhodes followed him through a patch of white, sandy loam. They bumped across a cattle guard and then followed the rutted trail for a quarter of a mile to where Bert had stacked the brush.

The brush was in three huge piles, ready for burning. Off to one side was Bert's tractor, with a front-end loader attached. Some of the brush had been cleared by hand, but most had been pulled or pushed up by the tractor and then stacked.

Bert stopped his pickup near one of the piles and got out. Rhodes stopped behind him. He could see the boxes even before he got out of his car. Whoever had put them there had made little or no attempt to hide them.

Bert was pointing when Rhodes walked up. "Right out in the open," Bert said.

"Hard to figure," Rhodes said, and it was. Though the foliage on the brush was scanty, the boxes could have been hidden easily if a little effort had been expended.

"Maybe they was in a hurry," Bert said.

"Maybe," Rhodes said. He was looking around in the white sand for tire tracks, though Bert had already driven over the road twice and Rhodes himself once. The sand was so dry and fine, however, that even the recent tracks had left no clear impressions.

"Well, I guess I might as well get to it," Rhodes said.

5

"I'll just stand over here if you don't need my help," Bert said. "I've looked in enough boxes to suit me already."

Rhodes didn't say anything. He reached in the right-hand pocket of his pants and took out his little Schrade-Walden knife and opened the blade. It wasn't a pig-sticker, but it was sharp enough to do the job. He walked over to one of the sealed boxes and slit the tape.

Inside were more body parts, carefully wrapped in plastic. Arms and legs.

Being careful not to touch the box with his hands, Rhodes used the tip of the knife blade to close the flaps. Then he stepped over to the third box and slit the tape. The flaps raised slightly, and he flipped them up with the knife blade. Arms and legs.

"I don't know what's happened here, Bert," Rhodes said, "but I can see that something's missing."

"I don't care about lookin'," Ramsey said.

"I don't blame you," Rhodes said. He pushed the box lid down with the knife. "I am going to have to ask you to help me, though. These boxes are evidence, just as much as what's in them. If you don't mind it too much, maybe we could load them in your truck and you could take them back to town for me."

"I guess I could do that," Bert said. "After all, I been haulin' parts around for a while already." He walked over to his truck, got in, and backed it up near the pile of brush.

When he got out, Rhodes said, "Just kind of grab the boxes by the edges. Try not to handle them too much."

Bert lowered the tailgate of the S-10. "I get it," he said. "Fingerprints."

"I doubt it," Rhodes said, "but it's a possibility."

They set the boxes on the tailgate and then slide them to the front of the bed near the cab.

"Where you plannin' to take these things?" Bert asked.

"Good question. I think we'll take them to Ballinger's. Clyde ought to know what to do with them if anybody does." Clyde Ballinger owned Clearview's oldest funeral home. In the course of his job, Rhodes had gotten to know him fairly well.

"Good idea," Ramsey said. "I'll meet you in the back."

Ballinger's Funeral Home had once been the home of one of Clearview's wealthiest citizens, and it was located on one of the town's main streets, conveniently near both a large Baptist church and the town's only hospital. Its immaculate grounds, shaded by huge oak trees, had once held Clearview's only private swimming pool and tennis courts. The pool had long since been filled in, and the tennis courts had been replaced with lawn grass.

The building itself was an impressive affair of red brick with a semicircular walk in front and large, white columns running the length of its fifty-foot porch. A side street led to the driveway, which in turn led to the rear entrance, the one through which most of Clyde Ballinger's clients, as he preferred to think of them, were admitted to his place of business.

Behind the main building was a much smaller house, also of brick, which had once served as servants' quarters. Now it was Ballinger's private office and retreat, a place where not just anyone was allowed to enter. Rhodes was one of the privileged ones, however, and he was there to explain to Ballinger about the three boxes sitting in the driveway.

"As you can see, Clyde," Rhodes was saying, "I've got a little problem here."

"Little's not the word I'd use," Ballinger said. His

voice boomed in the small living room where the two men sat. Everything Ballinger said was loud, except when he was engaged in the practice of his trade. He was, in fact, a very unlikely funeral director, or at least unlikely to anyone who thought morticians wore black suits and gloomy looks. Ballinger was short, fat, and dapper. He knew all the latest jokes, and he never wore black except to funerals.

"In fact," Ballinger said, "it looks to me like you got something that would even give the boys at the 87th a bad time."

Rhodes looked around the office at the bookshelves that lined three walls. They were filled with paperback books. Ballinger was an inveterate garage-sale shopper, and he bought nearly any crime-related paperback that he could find. One shelf was filled with old books by authors Rhodes had never heard of—Harry Whittington, Charles Williams, Jim Thompson, Gil Brewer. Another was devoted to John D. MacDonald and the 87th Precinct stories of Ed McBain. Rhodes had read a few of the latter, though he usually stuck to Louis L'Amour.

"I don't know, Clyde," Rhodes said. "Seems like crime stories in books are a lot worse than the real thing."

"Aw, come on," Ballinger said. "Parts of bodies dumped in a brush pile? Three boxes of parts? Hell, Sheriff, that's like something the Deaf Man would come up with. I remember one time—"

"Not now, Clyde," Rhodes said, cutting him off. He knew that if Ballinger got started telling about one of his favorite plots, they'd be there all day. "What I need right now is a place to store those boxes. And I need for you to keep quiet about what's in them."

Ballinger was clearly a little put out at not getting to tell his story, but he wasn't one to hold a grudge. "All right, Sheriff. All right. I got a nice cool place where you can put those things. But it's asking a lot to ask me to keep quiet about them. What am I going to tell Tom?"

Tom Skelly was Ballinger's partner, the one who did a lot of the actual work. Clyde was more or less the public relations side of the business. "You can tell Tom," Rhodes said. "But no one else. If this gets out, we'll have the biggest scare this county ever saw. It'll be like they were filming *The Texas Chainsaw Massacre* and everybody believed it was for real."

"I guess I can keep it quiet," Ballinger said. "You'd be surprised at the things I've had to hush up in this place. I remember the time that Old Lady Pinkston died—"

"Don't tell me," Rhodes said. "Remember, you hushed it up."

"Right," Ballinger said.

"I'll be sending someone over here later to fingerprint those boxes," Rhodes said.

"I'll tell Tom," Ballinger said. "I guess you want to move them into storage personally."

"That's right," Rhodes said.

"Well, let's get on with it." Ballinger stood up. "Did I ever tell you about that Jim Thompson book with the deputy sheriff in it? He's a psychotic killer, see—"

"Yeah, I think you told me about that one," said Rhodes, who had had some trouble with a deputy of his own fairly recently.

"It's a good one," Ballinger said as they went out the office door.

2

AFTER A HAMBURGER and a Dr. Pepper at the Blue
Bonnet cafe, Rhodes drove back to the jail. The arm was
still on his desk.

"I've got to take that thing over to Ballinger's," he
told Hack. "Any trouble while I was out?"

"Miz Thurman called," Hack said.

Rhodes waited. Hack told things at his own rate and in
his own way. There was no need to rush him. He worked
for the county practically free, and he did a fine job.
Rhodes was willing to put up with his approach to
reporting on calls.

"Said she was goin' blind again," Hack finally said.

"Who'd you send to change the bulb?" Rhodes asked.
Mrs. Thurman was nearly ninety and lived alone. Every
now and then a light bulb burned out in her kitchen or her
living room. When it happened, she called the sheriff's
office and said that she was going blind, that everything
was getting dark. After the first call, Rhodes had begun
sending over someone with a bulb.

"Sent the new deputy," Hack said. The new deputy
was a sore point with Hack.

"You know," Rhodes said, "I think that new Wal-
Mart is having a sale on those long-life bulbs. I ought to
buy a few and keep them in reserve for Mrs. Thurman."

"You ask me, you spoil that old woman," a new voice
put in. It was the jailer, Lawton, coming in from the cell
block.

"Who you callin' *old?*" Hack asked. "Miz Thurman's not much older'n you, you old buzzard."

Lawton was seventy, but he didn't look it. In fact, if Hack Jensen resembled Bud Abbott, Lawton looked a lot like Lou Costello, his face still almost baby-smooth, round, and chubby. "Maybe so," he said, "but she ain't got so much on you, either." Then he happened to look over at Rhodes's desk. "Godamighty," he said. "What's that?"

"Just what you think it is," Rhodes said. "That's all I know, though."

"What's the county comin' to, I wonder?" Lawton said. "I ain't never seen anything like that on a sheriff's desk before."

"There's more where that came from," Hack said. "Ain't that right, sheriff?"

"That's right," Rhodes replied. "But that's something you'll have to keep to yourselves."

"I guess we know how to do that," Hack said.

"I'm going to take that thing over to Ballinger's," Rhodes said. "Send the new deputy"—now he was doing it, he thought—"Send the new deputy over there with a fingerprint kit. I don't expect we'll find anything, but we've got to give it a try." He carefully picked up the arm and carried it out to the car.

He drove toward Ballinger's, thinking about the new deputy. He thought she was working out fine, but Hack and Lawton didn't approve. The idea of a woman deputy was almost too much for them, and they couldn't even bring themselves to call her by her name, which happened to be Ruth Grady.

Rhodes had been surprised when she applied for the job, but she was certainly qualified for it. She'd been to a community college near Houston and gotten an associates degree in law enforcement, which required her to work for a local law enforcement agency twenty hours a week for two semesters. Then she'd worked for a little police department in South Texas for a couple of years. The climate had been too humid and disagreeable for her, however, and she'd moved to Clearview to live with her bedridden father. Her father had died a few weeks before the episode that had involved Rhodes's former deputy, Johnny Sherman. When she found out about the vacancy on Rhodes's staff, she had applied.

Rhodes himself had been skeptical at first, but she was qualified for the job, certainly more qualified than anyone else who had applied, and he had hired her. Hack and Lawton were not pleased.

Rhodes left the arm at the funeral home with the others, told Clyde that Ruth Grady would be the one coming to do the fingerprinting, and drove home. Saturday afternoon was generally a slow time for the forces of law and order in Blacklin County. The business people were hard at work trying to earn a few dollars, and those who had the day off were at home relaxing and having a beer or taking a nap—maybe watching a little television. Saturday night was a different story, but for the time being things were quiet.

Rhodes pulled up in his driveway and called Hack on the radio to let him know where he'd be. "Have the new . . . have Ruth call me if she finds anything at Ballinger's," he said.

"I'll do it," Hack said. "She took care of Miz Thurman, and she'll be over to Ballinger's pretty soon."

Rhodes got out of the car. Thanks to the August heat and the lack of rain, his yard was covered with brown, dry grass. He figured that he'd let nature take its course; if it rained, the yard got water. Otherwise, it didn't. The grass would have to fend for itself. Rhodes hated yard work. Besides, if the grass died, that meant he didn't have to mow it. The appearance of the yard had gone downhill considerably since his daughter, Kathy, had taken a teaching job in Richardson. She had left three weeks before to find an apartment and get settled, and the yard missed her already.

For that matter, Rhodes missed her, too. Since his wife, Claire, had died, Kathy had more or less taken care of him, not that he wasn't capable of taking care of himself. But her involvement with Johnny Sherman and his own involvement—if that's what it was, he thought—with Ivy Daniel had combined to make her decide that it was time to leave. Rhodes was glad, in a way, because she had a lot to offer the teaching profession. Still, the old house was empty without her.

He wandered into the living room and turned on the television set. John Wayne was just returning Natalie Wood to her family, after having searched relentlessly for her for years. Everyone in the family embraced and went inside their cabin, leaving John Wayne to stand alone on the porch outside. Rhodes knew how he felt. Then his mind drifted to the catch-phrase that the Duke had spoken throughout the movie: "That'll be the day." He thought about the Buddy Holly song that phrase had inspired and immediately felt better. One of these days he was going to dig out all his old 45 rpm records and play them for Ivy Daniel.

He thought about Ivy for a minute and wondered if she was old enough to remember Buddy Holly. He thought she probably was, but her age was something they'd never discussed. He decided not to bring it up when he played the records.

He remembered that the records were in the back of the hall closet in a cardboard box. He was moving coats and sweaters out of the way when the telephone rang.

It was Ruth Grady. "I'm over at Ballinger's, Sheriff," she said. "I think you'd better come over here if you can."

"I'll be there in a minute," Rhodes said. The records could wait.

Ruth Grady was short and compact. "Chunky" was the word that Hack had used, though not in her hearing. She had short, brown hair and wore a western-style straw hat. There was a short-barreled .38 in a holster at her waist, and she looked every inch a law officer, even if she was only sixty-four inches tall.

"I found it when I opened the second box," she said, showing Rhodes a yellow tag. Written on the tag was a man's name, Frank Royster.

"Somebody identifying the victims?" Rhodes said. "That's a new one."

They were standing in one of Ballinger's back rooms, the boxes open in front of them.

"Not exactly," Ruth said. "That tag is for identification, all right, but it wasn't put there by any crazed axe murderer or anything like that. It's the kind of tag they use to identify amputated limbs."

Rhodes hadn't been to the same school that Ruth had attended, but he caught on quickly. "I had a feeling all along that this wasn't a murder case," he said. "It's just a little too bizarre for Blacklin County."

"I guess you're right," Ruth said, "but we still have a lot of arms and legs here. They have to be disposed of somehow."

"Ballinger may be able to take care of that for us," Rhodes said. "That still leaves us with a case of illegal dumping, though. I thought hospitals were supposed to dispose of things like that."

Ruth hitched up her gun. "They are. I think we better talk to Mr. Ballinger."

Clyde Ballinger was obviously disappointed. "I thought we had a really good case going here," he said. "Well, who knows. Maybe something will turn up."

"I hope not," Rhodes said.

"Yeah. Well, I'd like to help you get rid of those things, but I can't," Ballinger said.

"You can't?" Ruth asked.

"Don't know if it'd be legal. Don't know what the owners, so to speak, might think about it. It's customary in some cases to bury the amputated part in the grave where the owner's going to have his eternal rest; that is, it's customary if he's reserved a plot somewhere." Ballinger was beginning to sound more like a funeral director.

"I thought hospitals burned them," Rhodes said.

"Oh, they do, in lots of cases. I can't figure why these turned up here," Ballinger said.

"I think we'd better get in touch with the owners of that land," Rhodes said. "I'm still not sure all this is on the up and up."

"You might be able to get somebody on a health violation," Ballinger said, "but I'm not sure there's any state law about dumping body parts on private property."

"He's probably right," Ruth said. "I think there's a law about public dumping grounds, though."

"This is ridiculous," Rhodes said. "Ruth, go on back to the jail and see if you can get in touch with Bert Ramsey. Get the phone number of the people who own that land where he found these things. If he doesn't have the number, go on over to the courthouse and find out the full name and get the number from information. I'm going to see what Dr. White has to say about all this."

"All right," Ruth said. "Will you be checking with me later?"

"As soon as I talk to Dr. White," Rhodes said. They left Ballinger's office and headed for their separate cars.

Dr. Sam White was the county health officer, a job he did more or less for free since he was seldom required to do anything. The rest of the time he took care of his herd of

15

registered Longhorn cattle, having retired from his medical practice a few years previously.

Rhodes located White in the pasture not far from his rambling brick home. He was sitting in his pickup looking over his herd when Rhodes drove up behind him.

"They look pretty good to me, Doctor," Rhodes said. The cattle were of all colors, but mostly red. Their horns weren't really long, at least not as long as one might expect from the name. They were all slick and well-fed.

"Yes, they surely do," Dr. White said. "What's on your mind, Sheriff?"

Rhodes told him.

"Well, it doesn't take an expert to tell you that such things are a definite health hazard," the doctor said. "They should certainly be disposed of as quickly as possible."

Rhodes told him why there would be a delay.

"I can see the legal problems, of course. No death certificates. Still, one would think . . ."

"No use in thinking," Rhodes said. "Ballinger won't do it."

"Then I suggest that you call the state Health Department," Dr. White said. "I have to admit that I've never heard of anything exactly like this before."

Rhodes shook his head. "Me neither," he said. "Me neither."

Back at the jail, Lawton was nowhere in sight, which was usually the case when "the new deputy" was in the office. Hack was sticking close to his radio and not talking. Rhodes asked Ruth Grady what she'd learned.

"Not much," she told him. "The property is owned by a man named Charles Dalton Adams, and he lives at 6616 Springalong in Houston. But I can't get him on the telephone."

"Great," Rhodes said. "And I can just imagine trying

to get in touch with the state Health Department on a Saturday afternoon."

"Dr. White can't do anything?" Ruth asked.

"He would if he could, I think," Rhodes said. "He's just as mixed up by all this as we are."

At this point Hack could not resist talking. "If Bert Ramsey'd just burned those boxes like he ought, there wouldn't be any trouble," he said.

Rhodes had to admit that Hack had a point. "I'll talk to Ballinger again tomorrow," he said. "I'm afraid this is going to be a real mess."

"Listen," said Hack, "it's Saturday night comin' up. If this is the worst mess you have, you can count yourself lucky."

That was two points for Hack, Rhodes decided, but he hoped nothing really bad came up. He was hoping to see Ivy.

"I'm going on home," he said. "You call me if anything bad happens. Otherwise, well . . ."

"I know, I know," Hack said. "Otherwise, leave you the hell alone. Pardon my French, ma'am." He looked at Ruth for the first time.

She smiled at him. "Don't mind me," she said. "I'm going home, too. Shift is nearly over. I'll try to get in touch with that Adams fella again tomorrow. I ought to be able to catch him home on Sunday."

"Good idea," Rhodes said. He left, hoping for a quiet evening at home.

He got it. He even got to play his Buddy Holly records for Ivy Daniel. All in all it was as relaxing an evening as he'd spent for several months.

He wouldn't have enjoyed it so much, however, if he'd known that at approximately ten o'clock somebody was blowing Bert Ramsey apart with a shotgun.

3

PEOPLE WHO HAD never been to Texas were often surprised by places like Blacklin County. They thought of Texas in terms of the densely populated Houston and Dallas/Fort Worth areas, never dreaming that within a few hours' drive of either city there could be an entire county of an approximately 150-square-mile area that was home to a mere twenty thousand or so people. It seemed impossible, but there it was. And Blacklin County was not a rarity.

What was rare in the county was murder. In Houston, folks were disappointed if their nightly news didn't inform them of a murder or two every day, but then Houston's population was considerably larger than that of Blacklin County. More than one hundred times larger, in fact.

There was crime in Blacklin County, of course. That very Saturday night, there were people arrested for speeding, for driving while intoxicated, and for disturbing the peace. Someone drove away from a convenience store without paying for a tank of gas. Someone spray-painted the concrete sides of a railroad underpass only a mile from the city limits of Clearview with the words SENIORS FOREVER 1988. There was nothing unusual about things like that.

Murder was unusual. But at ten o'clock that Saturday night, no one knew that murder was being committed. No one, that is, except for Bert Ramsey and the killer.

Rhodes didn't find out the time until later, after an autopsy had been performed on what was left of Bert

Ramsey. The time wasn't exact, but it was as close as the doctor could come.

When he thought about it later, Rhodes wondered what he might have been doing at ten o'clock. He'd called Ivy Daniel, who'd agreed to have supper with him, and he'd picked her up about seven.

They went to the Taco and Tamale, a Mexican food cafe that had recently opened in what had been an old house. Rhodes liked the hot sauce especially, because it was just hot enough without burning all the skin off the inside of his mouth. They had tacos and tamales.

Then they went to Rhodes's house to listen to the records. Ivy admitted that she dimly recalled Buddy Holly, and Rhodes was pleased that she remembered "Rave On" and "Not Fade Away," two of his own favorites. For his money, Elvis wasn't really the king. Buddy Holly was. But then, Holly hadn't lived to get fat and turn into a Las Vegas entertainer.

"What else have you got in that box?" Ivy asked after he played both the "A" and "B" sides of all the Buddy Holly records.

Rhodes pulled out a handful of records. "Have a look," he said.

Ivy took the flat 45s. "Fats Domino," she said. "The Everly Brothers. Elvis. Gene Vincent. This is quite a collection you have here. Play some of these."

Rhodes put on Fats Domino, stacking up "Blue Monday," "Valley of Tears," and "Ain't That a Shame."

"Let's dance," he said, and then couldn't believe he'd said it. He hadn't even been much of a dancer when the records were popular, and he certainly hadn't been doing much dancing in the nearly thirty years since.

It was too late to say anything, though, because Ivy was in his arms and moving around the floor. He tried to lead, and to his surprise he found that he was actually dancing. Or at least doing a pretty fair imitation.

When Rhodes had met Ivy about four months before,

he hadn't really thought anything would come of it. She was running for justice of the peace in the May primary, and he was running for sheriff. They had been brought together again by a case that Rhodes had been working on, and he had found her quite attractive. He knew that she was nearly as old as he was, old enough to remember Buddy Holly, but her china-doll face made her look younger. It was also misleading, because she was not nearly as fragile as she appeared.

Rhodes had won the primary election and would be running unopposed in November, much to his surprise considering the events just before the voting. Ivy, however, had not won, a fact that both she and Rhodes attributed to male prejudice against women justices, something that the county just wasn't ready for yet.

Ivy had a good job in an insurance office and didn't take her defeat too badly, but she was disappointed. She made it clear that she would try again.

On his side, Rhodes was just grateful that they had met. Since his wife had died, he had not developed an interest in any woman. Not that a few hadn't tried. Ivy had changed all that, however. He was definitely interested in her. He was sure she was interested in him, too, but he wasn't being pushy about it. He'd grown up before the sexual revolution and had no interest in participating in it at this late date. Or at least that's what he kept telling himself. Dancing with Ivy was beginning to change his mind.

Then "Ain't That a Shame" dropped onto the turntable, and the dancing came to a halt. "No way," Rhodes laughed. "No way. That fast dancing is too much like work."

They put a few more of Rhodes's records on the spindle and then sat on the couch. "So what's new in the law and order business?" Ivy asked.

Rhodes laughed. He had become quite comfortable

20

with Ivy and often discussed the cases he was working on with her. Most things were like Mrs. Thurman's light bulbs, so she was hardly expecting to be told about boxes of arms and legs.

"But that's terrible," she said after Rhodes had finished the story. "And no one will bury them?"

"Not Clyde Ballinger, anyway," Rhodes said. "I think he's afraid of a lawsuit."

"But surely they ought to be disposed of decently!"

"I agree," Rhodes said. "But now they're evidence, I think."

"You *think!*"

"Well, we're not sure a crime has been committed. I mean, if all those limbs are legitimate amputations, then there may not be anything wrong with dumping them. I'm going to try to get in touch with the state Health Department, but there's not a hope of doing that until Monday."

"Of course there's something wrong with dumping them!" Ivy said. There was a spot of color high on each of her cheekbones, now. "It's . . . it's *indecent.*"

Rhodes didn't have anything to say to that for a minute. In the background the record changer clicked and dropped another disc. Ricky Nelson started singing "Hello, Mary Lou."

"I admit it's indecent," Rhodes finally said. "But indecent and illegal aren't always the same things. Still, I *would* like to know who put those boxes there, and why."

Ivy wasn't satisfied with that, he could tell, but she dropped the subject. He took her home shortly after eleven o'clock. By then, Bert Ramsey had been dead for nearly an hour.

The body was found by Bert's mother, who stopped by his house on her way to church. She called the jail, and

21

Hack Jensen called Rhodes, who arrived on the scene twenty minutes after the call.

Bert Ramsey had lived in Eller's Prairie, a place that was loosely defined as a "community." That meant, in Blacklin County, that there were six or seven houses along the three or four dirt roads that intersected where the Eller's Prairie Baptist Church stood. None of the houses was nearer than a half mile to another. No one named Eller had lived in any of them within living memory, and the nearest prairie was a couple of hundred miles away. Not that anyone in Blacklin County was bothered by the discrepancy.

The house where Bert had lived stood back from the road about fifty yards and was shaded by three large oaks. The blue S-10 pickup was parked in a shed a few yards from the house. Beside it was a space probably occupied most of the time by the tractor Rhodes had seen the day before. The yard around the house was neatly mowed and very green, one of the benefits of having well water and not having to pay a city water bill.

Rhodes parked behind a thirty-year-old Ford Tudor with a light blue body and a navy top. There were large areas of rust on the trunk lid. Standing by the front door of the house was Mrs. Ramsey.

Mrs. Ramsey was a considerable woman. Rhodes guessed her weight at around 275 pounds, and he glanced involuntarily at the Ford to see if its springs sagged toward the driver's side. He thought it did, but that might have been his imagination.

Mrs. Ramsey was swathed in a navy blue dress, and she looked to Rhodes a little like Marjorie Main might have looked if she'd let herself go. She carried a worn leather purse in one hand and an even more thoroughly worn Bible in the other. It was still an hour before noon, so the heat hadn't reached its full power as yet, but Mrs. Ramsey's dress showed dark, circular stains under each armpit. When Rhodes reached her, he could see that she'd been crying. Her red eyes didn't help her appearance much.

"Buster Cullens done it," she said wearily when Rhodes reached her. "Ain't no doubt but that Buster done it."

"How's that, Mrs. Ramsey?" Rhodes said.

"Buster Cullens done it," she said again. "Ever since Wyneva took up with Buster, she's been after him to do it."

"Wyneva?" Rhodes asked.

"Wyneva Greer. She and Bert lived in sin here for six months. Then she left and took up with Buster Cullens. He's the one who done it."

It couldn't be put off any longer. "Did what?" Rhodes asked.

Mrs. Ramsey pushed open the screen door. Bert, or what was left of him, lay just inside it. His head was easily identifiable, but there wasn't much of his chest that hadn't been blasted into a red mass of blood and mangled flesh. Mrs. Ramsey let the door swing shut. For the first time, Rhodes noticed the flies that had clustered on the screen. Some of them had gotten inside.

Neither Rhodes nor Mrs. Ramsey said anything for a moment. The Eller's Prairie Baptist Church was about half a mile down the road. It had no air conditioning, and through its open windows came the strains of the opening hymn. Rhodes recognized it: "Amazing Grace." He didn't look at Mrs. Ramsey. "How did you call the jail?" he asked.

Mrs. Ramsey gestured vaguely in the direction of the rear of the house. "I went in the back door," she said.

"Did you call anyone else?"

"No," she said. "Just the jail."

"Let's go back in there," Rhodes said. "I have to make some calls, and we can call one of your friends."

"All of my friends will be in church," she said.

"Well, you can sit down while I call," Rhodes told her. He started around to the back, and Mrs. Ramsey followed slowly.

Inside the house, Rhodes walked through the kitchen to the living room. There was a huge Sony television set against one wall, with a Super Beta video recorder sitting in a cabinet beside it, along with a compact disc player. There were two La-Z-Boy chairs and a large, comfortable-looking couch, all sitting on a very thick, brown carpet. There was no telephone.

Mrs. Ramsey sank down in one of the chairs and immediately cranked up the footrest. "Lets me get the weight off me feet," she explained in a dead voice. "The phone's in the bedroom." She pointed to a door on Rhodes's left.

Rhodes entered the bedroom, which was dominated by a king-size waterbed. There was another television set and another VCR in that room. A red push-button phone sat on the night table beside the bed. Rhodes walked across the plush carpet, wishing he'd remembered to dust off his shoes before coming in the house.

First he called the justice of the peace, then the ambulance. Then he called Hack Jensen. "Get hold of Ruth Grady," he said. "Tell her I want her to footprint and fingerprint every arm and leg in those three boxes. We've got to make sure we can account for all of them one way or another."

Hack said he'd get right on it, and Rhodes went to look at the body of Bert Ramsey. He'd seen shotgun wounds before, and he already knew just about what he'd find. Whoever had shot Bert had been very close to him, so close that the pattern of shot hadn't had time to spread out before it hit him in the chest. He couldn't locate any stray pellets, so he figured that the shot had come from only a couple of feet away. Bert must have gone to the door and been shot almost as soon as he opened it, unless he had known whoever was there. Then he might have stood there for a while, talking.

Rhodes went back to the living room, where Mrs. Ramsey still sat in the La-Z-Boy chair. She had put her purse and Bible on the floor beside her and was wiping her eyes with a handkerchief.

"Mrs. Ramsey," Rhodes said. She made another brief wiping motion and wadded the handkerchief in her hand.

"Yes, Sheriff?"

"This Buster Cullens. Where does he live? He from around here?"

"He lives down on the Long Bridge road," Mrs. Ramsey said. "You go on past the church and turn right at the old hay barn. It's about two miles to the Long Bridge Crossing. He's livin' on the Kersey place."

"I know where that is," Rhodes said. "What makes you think he's the kind of man to do something like this?" Rhodes hated asking these questions, especially at a time like this, but he knew it was something that had to be done.

"He's a hard man," Mrs. Ramsey said. "Bert wasn't a hard man, Sheriff. He liked to work, and he was honest and fair. Anybody'd tell you that about him. Buster Cullens ain't like that."

"How do you mean?" Rhodes asked.

"He hangs out with a mean crowd. He rides a motor-sickle. . . ." Mrs. Ramsey's eyes seemed to unfocus momentarily as she stared off into the vague distance of her thoughts.

"Mrs. Ramsey?"

She snapped her attention back to Rhodes. "It was Buster that done it," she said with renewed conviction. "Listen, Sheriff, I live down past the church, too, not but a quarter mile past that old hay barn. Last night I heard motorsickles! I know that was it! All the rumblin', roarin', and poppin' like they do, it had to be motorsick-les! It was Buster Cullens!" She grabbed the handle on the right side of the chair and snapped it up, causing the footrest to drop. It was almost as if the chair had pro-pelled her to her feet. She scooped up her Bible and purse. "It was Buster Cullens," she repeated.

Just then the ambulance arrived. "Sit down for a few more minutes, Mrs. Ramsey," Rhodes said. "There's a few things I have to do."

She sank into the chair again, and Rhodes left the room.

Later, after the ambulance and the J.P. were gone, Rhodes went back inside to talk to Mrs. Ramsey once more, but she had nothing to add to what she'd already told him. He offered to drive her to the church, but she said, no, she'd rather go in her own car. He walked her outside and watched her get in the old Ford. The driver's side sagged and the springs groaned. Under other cir-cumstances, Rhodes might have thought it was funny.

She pulled the door shut, and Rhodes stepped over to the car. "Did you hear anything else last night?" he asked.

"No, Sheriff, I didn't," she said. "I know what you mean, but I didn't hear a thing, except for them motor-sickles. And I guess my house is just about the closest one to here." She started the car and circled around by the shed, then drove away.

Rhodes watched her go. The fact that she hadn't heard any gunshots didn't necessarily mean anything. She could have had the television set turned up, or she could have been asleep. He watched the old Ford travel down the road, dust pluming up behind it. It turned into the churchyard just as the first people were coming out the door. Maybe she would find some comfort there, Rhodes thought. He went back into the house.

There was nothing where Bert Ramsey had died to tell Rhodes anything, but he intended to search a little further. There was no evidence that anyone else had looked through the rooms, and therefore, it seemed likely that robbery wasn't the reason for the killing. So Rhodes decided to see what he could find.

It didn't take him long. In the back of a dresser drawer, rolled up in a sock, there was nearly six thousand dollars.

4

RHODES DROVE THE county car across Long Bridge, a
rickety wooden structure that really wasn't very long at
all. It had gotten its name from a certain Mr. Long, who
had built the original bridge at this crossing nearly a
hundred years ago. Rhodes knew this because he'd once
read a book on the history of Blacklin County. He
doubted that there was anyone else in the county—well,
maybe there were two or three others—who either knew,
or cared. Most of them didn't even know the bridge was
there.

The Kersey place was a quarter of a mile past the
bridge. There was a barbed wire fence with what people
called a "gap" in it, a gate made of barbed wire that
looked like part of the fence. Off the road twenty or
thirty yards was a house.

Rhodes got out of his car and opened the gap, then got
back in and drove through. He didn't bother to close it.

The house was old and weathered. It had been painted
once, no doubt, but that had been many years ago. No
trace of the original color remained. The boards were
weathered a uniform light gray. The roof looked to be in
pretty fair shape; it was probably no more than thirty or
so years old. Nearly all the windows that Rhodes could
see had glass in them, except for one on the front corner,
which had a pane missing.

The house was small, probably four rooms, Rhodes
guessed, and small ones at that. Out back there was
another very small house, which Rhodes recognized

immediately as the privy. It was made of the same weathered boards as the main house.

Beside the house, under the scanty shade of a huge mesquite tree, there was a black motorcycle. Rhodes knew nothing at all about motorcycles, but he could see the *Nighthawk* on the gas tank, along with the word *Honda*. From what he recalled of *The Wild One*, Marlon Brando had ridden a Harley-Davidson.

The house sat up on wooden blocks, and as Rhodes stepped toward the porch, a brownish dog that must have had a collie in its ancestry came out from the cool shadows beneath the house. It gave a half-hearted growl and its fur ruffled slightly, but that was all. It looked at Rhodes incuriously for a moment, then turned around, got down on its belly, and crawled back under the house.

"Mighty fine watchdog I got myself there," said a voice from the front doorway. Rhodes, whose attention had been on the dog, looked up. A man pushed open a half-collapsed screen door and looked back at him.

The man was big, that was all Rhodes thought at first. His shoulders were so wide they almost filled the doorway. He was wearing only a pair of black shorts, so that Rhodes could see the full expanse of his chest. He was also handsome, and Rhodes thought he looked a little like Reg Park in *Hercules in the Haunted World*.

There was a difference, though. This man's hands were hard and rough, and the callouses and creases were black from ground-in grease and carbon, the way a mechanic's hands are likely to get. He looked perfectly capable of dismantling an engine with his bare hands and maybe a small screwdriver.

"Your name Buster Cullens?" Rhodes asked.

"That's right," the man said, making no move to step out onto the porch. He didn't appear the least impressed by Rhodes's badge. "What's yours?" His voice, instead of the deep bass that would have seemed appropriate to

Rhodes, was thin, high and nasal. He sounded like Arnold Stang.

"I'm Sheriff Dan Rhodes. I'd like to talk with you for a minute."

Cullens stepped onto the porch. "All right," he said. "Talk."

"I'd like to talk to Wyneva Greer, too, if she's here," Rhodes said.

The man just looked at him. His eyes were black and set deep in their sockets.

Rhodes looked back. He didn't particularly care for macho games, but he could play them if he had to.

After about a minute, Cullens turned his head and yelled through the screen door. "Wyneva! Come out here if you're decent."

The screen door opened and a woman came out. Rhodes wasn't sure she was decent. She had on a pair of cut-off jeans, cut off so high that they must have hurt her when she walked. She was also wearing a faded denim vest. But she wasn't wearing a shirt. Rhodes looked down, then to the side. Then, deciding that she was playing a game too, he looked up.

Her hair was long and black, and her face was very pretty in a tough sort of way. She shrugged her shoulders, and her breasts jiggled behind the faded denim.

"So talk," Cullens said.

Rhodes cleared his throat as quietly as he could. "A neighbor of yours got himself killed last night," he said.

Cullens laid a proprietary arm on the woman's shoulders. "Sorry to hear that," he said. "Who was it?"

"Bert Ramsey," Rhodes said, looking at the woman, who gave no sign that the name meant anything to her. "I think Miss Greer knew him at one time. I'd like to know if you two saw or heard anything unusual last night."

Cullens didn't answer the question. "How'd he die?" he asked.

Rhodes had to admit that Cullens was smart. Either that, or he was completely innocent. He was certainly asking the right questions, the ones that made it appear as if he knew nothing at all about what had happened. Rhodes saw no harm in answering him.

"Someone cut him down with a shotgun," Rhodes said, cutting a glance at Wyneva Greer out of the corner of his eye. She appeared completely unaffected.

"Too bad," Cullens said, as if he didn't feel it was too bad at all. In fact, he said it so casually it was as if death, or at least someone else's death, was a matter that didn't concern him in the least. "Naw," he said then, "we didn't hear a thing last night."

"I suppose you were both here all evening?" Rhodes asked.

Cullens looked at Wyneva, and for the first time Rhodes saw an emotion flit briefly across her face. It was fear, he was pretty sure of that.

"Yeah," Cullens said. "We were right here. That right, Wyneva?"

The woman nodded slowly. "That's right," she said. Her voice was low and husky. She didn't meet Rhodes's eyes.

"How'd you two come to be staying in such an out-of-the-way place, anyway?" Rhodes asked.

Cullens looked as if he might say it was none of Rhodes's business, but if the thought had crossed his mind, he didn't speak it aloud. "One of the Kerseys is a cousin of mine," he said. "When I decided to come up here from Houston, he let me have the loan of it till I could get a good mechanic's job somewhere. I haven't found one yet."

Rhodes looked again at Cullens's hands. He might not have had a job, but it was a cinch that he'd been doing some mechanic work somewhere.

"Well," said Rhodes, "I appreciate you all taking the

31

time to talk to me. I might have to come back by in case I think of something else to ask."

Cullens just looked at him, so Rhodes got in his car, started it, and drove to the gap. After he drove through, he looked back at the house. Cullens was still standing on the porch, watching him, but Wyneva was nowhere in sight. Rhodes closed the gap. The dog came out from under the house again, and Rhodes drove away.

On his way back to Clearview, Rhodes stopped at Bert Ramsey's house again. This time he looked around the tractor shed, but he couldn't find anything else of interest.

He took off his hat and waved it in front of his face, trying to stir up a little breeze. It was early afternoon, now, the hottest part of the day.

About three hundred yards in back of Ramsey's house, there was a thick line of trees. Rhodes wondered just how far back Ramsey's property ran, and he wondered if there might be a stock tank somewhere in those woods. He'd like to go bass fishing in a little tank that no one had tried out yet.

He'd also like to know a lot more about Bert Ramsey. It seemed to Rhodes that Ramsey had been around Clearview for at least ten years, doing odd jobs and such. And before that he was in the army, or at least that was the way Rhodes remembered it. Say he was around thirty-five years old. Not particularly good-looking, weathered from plenty of hard work in the outdoors, quiet, never in trouble with the law.

How, Rhodes wondered, did a man like that manage to afford two new TV sets and two VCRs? How did a man like that manage to have nearly six thousand dollars in very large bills stuffed in his sock drawer? And why was he dead?

Rhodes settled his hat back on his head and walked to

the car. He was a patient man, and he would start asking questions. He wanted to talk to Mrs. Ramsey again, and he wasn't through with Buster Cullens and Wyneva Greer, not by a long shot. He often envied the big-city police departments that he read about, with their computers and ballistics experts—not that a ballistics expert would be any help with a shotgun killing. He had to work differently from them. He had to talk to people and sift the facts from the lies. If he was careful and if he kept it up long enough, he usually got results, even if he wasn't in the 87th Precinct.

He got in the car and drove back to town.

Clyde Ballinger was ecstatic. "Boy, Sheriff Rhodes, this is a good one!" he exclaimed. "Carella and Hawes would love this! I mean, you've got hacked limbs, you've got a murder that's connected, you've got—"

"Wait a minute," Rhodes interrupted. He was beginning to regret stopping by Ballinger's to check on how Ruth Grady was doing with her fingerprinting. "We don't know that there's any connection at all. In fact, there probably isn't. We'll know more when we get in touch with the owners of the old Caster place."

"Come on, Sheriff," Ballinger said. "There's always a connection in cases like this. I remember one time when this dead woman—she was buck naked—was found right across the street from the 87th. And right after that, the guys started getting this weird series of clues about something that looked totally unrelated. Anyway—"

"Anyway," Rhodes cut in, "this isn't New York."

"Isola," Ballinger said.

"Whatever," Rhodes said. "We're just a small county where things like that don't happen."

"I don't believe it," Ballinger said. "I bet some guy has been hacking up bodies, and Ramsey was disposing of them for him. I bet his conscience got the better of him and he came to you. But he just couldn't bring himself to tell the whole story. And then, when the hacker found out what Ramsey had done, he killed him. I bet that's just the way it was!"

Rhodes sighed and changed the subject. "Why aren't you assisting in the autopsy?" he asked.

"I don't do that sort of thing much these days," Ballinger said. "Always glad to allow the use of the facilities, though. Afraid you won't learn much from this one."

"I'm just hoping for an estimated time of death," Rhodes said. "Have you seen Deputy Grady today?"

"She's in there doing her job. I haven't bothered her."

"I think I'll just walk on over and have a word with her. See you later, Clyde."

"Sure, Sheriff. As soon as I get in touch with Mrs. Ramsey and arrange for the funeral, I'll let you know."

"Thanks," Rhodes said. He wasn't sure that he'd learn anything by attending Bert Ramsey's funeral, but he wasn't going to take a chance by missing it. He left Ballinger's office and walked over to the back room of the funeral home where Ruth Grady was working.

Clearview didn't have a morgue, but the back room of Ballinger's was close enough. It was quite cold; there was no danger of putrefaction Ballinger had kept bodies in there for days, when necessary.

Ruth was just finishing her job. There was a neat stack of fingerprint cards on a small table, but all the various limbs had been replaced in their boxes. Rhodes wasn't sure just how much good the prints would do. He could eventually send them through the necessary channels, but he couldn't do it over the telephone, or whatever the big-city boys did. Besides, he was hoping to clear up the whole mess when he got in touch with the Adamses.

Ruth looked up when he walked in. "Hello, Sheriff," she said, seemingly cheerful in spite of the grisly nature

34

of her assigned job. "I'm afraid I've got some bad news."

"Let's hear it."

"Well, it was easy enough to get fingerprints and even footprints. That part's OK. The bad news is that there aren't any other prints. Not on the boxes, not on the plastic, not on the tape. Whoever did this was wearing gloves."

"Surgical gloves, I'd bet," Rhodes said. "Did you find any more of those tags?"

"Sure did." She reached down to the table and picked up a stack of the yellow tags from beside the fingerprint forms. "I went ahead and wrote the names from the tags on a piece of paper and stuck it on the limbs."

"Good job," Rhodes said. "I'll take this stuff back to the jail, and you can go out on patrol for a while. I'm going to give this Adams guy a call and see if he can tell us what's going on."

"Anything new on the disposal?" Ruth asked.

"No," Rhodes said. "I'm sure I can get in touch with the state Health Department tomorrow and clear things up. That is, if all these things are legitimate."

"I hope so. If there's not a law against dumping something like this, there certainly ought to be."

"Remember," Rhodes said, "these boxes were on private property. That makes a difference."

"Hack told me about Bert Ramsey," Ruth said. "Any connection there?"

Rhodes concealed his surprise. It was hard for him to believe that Hack had told Ruth anything that he didn't have to tell her. Maybe he was softening. "Not as far as I know," he said. "There could be, but for now we're going to treat this business as a separate incident. If we find a connection, then we'll see."

"Does that mean you have a suspect?"

"Not exactly," Rhodes said, shaking his head. "I

wouldn't say I have much of anything yet. You managed to find yourself any informants?

Ruth nodded slowly. "Maybe," she said. "One, anyway."

In a small county, informants—Rhodes had never liked to call them snitches—were just as important as they were in New York. Or Isola. Wherever. It was true that much of the gossip of the county could be heard through Hack or Lawton, who seemed to pick it up from the air, but there was nevertheless an underside of society whose comings and goings weren't part of the common talk. The more informants a deputy had, the better his (or her, Rhodes reminded himself) chances of picking up a piece of talk, a hint, a word or two, that just might prove to be the key to whatever case he was working at the time. Or even to a case that had almost been forgotten.

Rhodes didn't ask who Ruth's informant was. Each deputy cultivated his own sources, and each kept them private. Rhodes had a few sources of his own. Instead, he said, "See what you can find out about motorcycles."

"Motorcycles?"

"Yeah. Motorcycles. I'd like to know who's riding them these days."

Ruth looked puzzled, but she said, "I'll see what I can find out."

"If you hear anything, let me know," Rhodes said. He gathered up the cards and went back to his car. Ruth Grady was not far behind.

5

WHEN RHODES ARRIVED at the jail, the air conditioner was making a peculiar clanking noise.

"Compressor goin' out," Hack said gloomily. "I bet it goes out any minute, and we'll never get anybody in here to fix it on a Sunday. It'll be a hunnerd and twenty degrees in here by dark."

"Maybe it'll wait until Monday," Rhodes said. He looked over at the radio desk where the remains of a German chocolate cake rested on a paper plate. "What's that?" he asked.

"That's a cake," Hack said.

"I'm a keenly observant lawman," Rhodes said. "I can see it's a cake. Where did it come from?"

"Need to improve your interrogation techniques a little, though, don't you," Hack said, laughing. "Ru— the new deputy brought it by."

All right, thought Rhodes. Hack's not getting soft; he's just getting softened. But he didn't comment. "Anything new?" he asked.

"Not except for Bert Ramsey. The drunks've all gone home with their wives and lawyers. Last one left about an hour ago. Pretty quiet around here now."

"And that's it? Nothing going on at all?" If there was, Hack would tell him, but it sometimes seemed to take forever.

"That's it." Hack paused. "Except for the heart attack," he said finally.

"Heart attack?" Rhodes asked. "What heart attack?"

"Prisoner," Hack said. "Prisoner had a heart attack."

Rhodes controlled himself. "Oh," he said. "I thought maybe you or Lawton had had one."

"Not us," Lawton said, as he came through the doorway leading to the cell block. He was carrying a broom. "Me and Hack, why I guess we're healthy as a pair of mules."

"Healthier," Hack said. "I can't even remember the last time either one of us two had a cold, much less had to take a day off. I think it was in '81. Or maybe it was '82. I remember it was in October, though, I'm pretty sure of that. . . ."

"The prisoner," Rhodes said.

"Oh, yeah," Hack said. "Public Safety patrol car brought her in around midnight. Pretty little thing."

"What was the charge?" Rhodes asked.

"Speeding," Lawton said. "They lost her when she got that little Por-she of hers up over a hunnerd and thirty-five."

"Lost her?"

"Yeah, but they found her."

"Found her?"

Hack shook his head as if Rhodes were being especially dense. "She got a little scared about driving so fast, so she slowed down and turned in on one of the old oil field roads close to town. Must've waited in there till she thought the DPS was long gone and then came rollin' out. So they caught her."

"Yeah," Lawton said. "They wasn't gone at all. They was still patrollin' in the area, and when she came out of the oil field, they ran right up on her."

"Brought her in and charged her," Hack said. "She called a lawyer, and he come down early this mornin' and put up bond."

"What about the heart attack?" Rhodes asked.

"Oh, she had that right after she got here," Hack said.

"Fell right down on the floor and rolled her eyes and kicked a little bit and yelled that her time was comin'. Said she had a weak heart, and the police brutality had done her in."

"Wasn't much to it," Lawton said. "You remember old Billy Lee Tingley? Now, there was a guy who knew how to have a heart attack. I've seen him throw one or two right here in this room that would've fooled Dr. Denton Cooley his own self."

Hack smiled a reminiscent smile. "He could sure do it, all right. Whatever happened to him?"

"Got drunk one night and went to sleep on the railroad tracks down near Thurston," Lawton said. "Train killed him."

"About this prisoner," Rhodes said.

"Not much to tell," Hack said. "Betty Thornton was her name. She ought to have been ashamed of tryin' to fool two old hands like me and Lawton. I could do a better job myself."

"Gave that DPS boy a few bad minutes, though," Lawton said.

"Yeah, I didn't know him," Hack said. "He must be a new one. But he's smart. He caught on pretty quick when you tipped him."

"Yeah, and that young woman didn't try to carry it too far," Lawton said. "She even laughed a little about it. I hated to put her in a cell. It's not the nicest place in town."

"You give her the front one?" Rhodes asked. They kept the front cell for women prisoners. It was fairly clean, and it was private, separated from the others by a plywood wall.

"Right," said Lawton. "We took good care of her, Sheriff. You don't have to worry about that."

"Good," Rhodes said. "Now I'm going to make a phone call. Hack, get on the radio and talk to the DPS, see if that new fella's on patrol. Ask him if he's seen any motorcycles around lately. Same thing with Buddy and Bob."

"OK, Sheriff," Hack said.

Rhodes got through to Charles Adams without any trouble. As Adams talked, Rhodes could hear a television set in the background, with an announcer doing a play-by-play of an NFL exhibition game. When he told Adams what the problem was, the Houston man began to sputter.

"Damn," Adams said. "Damn, damn, damn."

"That's just about the way I feel, too," Rhodes told him, trying to get comfortable in his squeaky chair. "You don't think you could enlighten us any, do you?"

Adams hesitated, and Rhodes could hear the TV announcer clearly. Danny White of the Cowboys had just been sacked for a ten-yard loss by a Miami linebacker.

Finally, Adams spoke. "You got a brother-in-law, Sheriff?" he asked.

"No," Rhodes answered. "I surely don't."

"Well, I do," Adams said. "He's a doctor, an M.D. Works out of a little hospital not far from here up the interstate. We got to talking the other day, and I told him I was clearing some land, having the brush burned. He was real interested. Seems he was having this little disposal problem. . . ."

"I think I'm beginning to get the picture," Rhodes said. "Can you give me his name and number? I think I need to give him a call."

"Sure, I guess so. He . . . he's not in any trouble is he?" Adams hesitated. "Hell," he said, "I guess he must be in trouble or the sheriff wouldn't be calling. I mean *big* trouble. He isn't in big trouble, is he?"

"I'm not sure, to tell the truth," Rhodes said. "That's one of the reasons I need to talk to him."

"Well, all right," Adams said. He gave Rhodes the telephone number. "His name's Rawlings. Dr. Malcolm Rawlings."

Rhodes thanked Adams for his time and hung up. Just as he put the phone down, the air conditioner began to clank louder and faster.

"It's goin' out, I know it's goin' out," Hack said, shaking his head gloomily.

"Try to think positively," Rhodes said. "It might last through the night if you don't think too many negative thoughts."

"Sometimes I worry about you, Sheriff," Hack said. "I really do."

"I do, too," Rhodes said. "What about the DPS?"

"Not a thing," Hack said. "No motorsickles around, least not in a bunch. Not that the DPS knows about, anyway."

That information didn't really mean too much, Rhodes thought. There were plenty of places in Blacklin County where hundreds of people could hide if they were of a mind to.

"Ask Buddy and Bob when they come in," he said. "I've got to make another call, if I can hear anything over that racket."

"It's goin' out," Hack said.

Rhodes turned to the telephone.

Dr. Malcolm Rawlings was in, apparently watching the same game his brother-in-law had been tuned in to. Rhodes wasn't quite sure, because the air conditioner was making so much noise that he had difficulty hearing the background noise. He could hear Rawlings just fine, however. The man's voice boomed out when he answered the telephone. When Rhodes told him who he was and what he wanted, however, Rawlings got considerably quieter.

"Well, ah, you see, Sheriff, there's been a little problem here, and . . . well . . . ah . . ."

"Let's put it this way," Rhodes said. "Just answer yes or no. Did you put those boxes in that brush pile?"

"Well, now, Sheriff, there's a word you lawmen use . . . I think it's 'extenuating.' Yes," Rawlings said, sounding relieved, "that's it. 'Extenuating circumstances.' That's what we have here, Sheriff, a plain case of extenuating circumstances."

"Yes or no?" Rhodes said.

"Well, yes, I did put the boxes there, but there are extenuating circumstances," Rawlings said. Rhodes thought of Raymond Burr playing Perry Mason.

"Just exactly what *are* the circumstances?" Rhodes asked.

"Well, as you may know, Sheriff, we usually burn amputated limbs."

"I know," Rhodes said. He was getting a little tired of Rawlings's runaround. "But not in fields."

"Of course not," Rawlings said. He chuckled to show that he understood Rhodes's irony. "But I've been doing some work with tissue samples. That's why I had the limbs in the first place, you see. I certainly didn't do all those amputations in the little hospital, here. We're just not equipped. And in fact, that's the real problem. A lack of proper facilities. The furnace is just too small, frankly. It just wouldn't handle the job."

"So you decided to dump the remains," Rhodes said.

"Well, I, ah, wouldn't say 'dump.' I just wanted to dispose of them in an accepted and sanitary manner. They would have been burned, you know."

"There's just a little complication," Rhodes said. "The man who found those boxes is dead. Someone killed him last night."

There was a lengthy silence. Rhodes listened to the clanking of the air conditioner and snatches of the football game. Finally, Rawlings spoke again. "Do you think that this, ah, incident will get into the news media? I have a . . . a professional standing."

Rhodes thought of the Blacklin County news media. He thought of Clyde Ballinger. "It might," he said. "But that's beside the point. Right now, you're connected with a murder case, and that's more important than your 'professional standing.' Besides, there's the matter of proper disposal. I'll be talking to the state Health Department tomorrow about that problem."

"I see."

"No, Doctor, I don't think you really do," Rhodes said. He was trying not to lose his temper, but it wasn't easy. "I want you up here in my office tomorrow morning. I want a strict accounting of every single limb in those boxes. I want you to be able to prove where every one of them came from. And while you're at it, you might be giving a little thought to exactly where you were on Saturday night."

Rawlings sucked in his breath. "Are you accusing me . . . ?"

"Not at all," Rhodes said. "But I want you here in the morning at ten o'clock."

"But my patients!" Rawlings protested.

"Get someone to cover for you, or cancel your appointments," Rhodes said. "It's either that, or I get the Houston police to pick you up."

"I suppose I'll have to be there, then," Rawlings said reluctantly. He didn't sound happy.

"Fine," Rhodes said. "I'll see you at ten o'clock." He put the telephone down before Rawlings had time to reply. "Some people are more interested in covering their own backsides than in helping the law," he told Hack.

"What do you mean 'some people'?" Hack said. "You mean everybody."

Rhodes grinned. "You're right," he said.

The telephone rang, and Rhodes picked it up. It was Dr. White, calling from Ballinger's. "I can't tell you much, Sheriff," he said. "Not much to tell, really. Bert Ramsey died from a shotgun blast to the chest, fired at close range. I'd say not more than four or five feet. Double-ought buckshot. About ten P.M., depending on when he ate supper, which was steak and beans, mainly."

"That's it, huh?" Rhodes asked.

"Not exactly," White said. "There's one other little thing that might be of interest to you."

"What's that?"

"Ramsey had a tattoo," White said.

"I think he was in the army," Rhodes said. "I guess lots of guys get tattoos in the army."

"Not this kind," White told him. "I think I've seen a picture of one like it in the newspapers. It's a skeleton, riding a motorcycle."

"I've seen that, too," Rhodes said. "Los Muertos."

"That's what I thought," White said. "They've been in the news a lot lately."

"That's a fact," Rhodes said. "Thanks, Doctor."

"Anytime," White said. They hung up.

"What's that about Los Muertos?" Lawton asked.

"Bert Ramsey had one of their tattoos," Rhodes said.

No one said anything for a minute. They listened to the clanking and clattering of the air conditioner. Rhodes leaned back in his chair, causing it to squeak its high-pitched squeak.

"He'd been doing handyman work around here for a long time," Hack said at last.

"Seems to me that he was in the army before that," Lawton said. "Least, that's what I always heard."

"Makes you wonder if we heard wrong," Rhodes said. "I thought I remembered it that way, too. But maybe he wasn't in the army. Maybe he was just gone somewhere else. Maybe he was a member of a different organization."

"What's that mean, anyway, that 'Los Muertos'?" Hack asked.

"You ought to know that one," Lawton told him. "You must be gettin' old. Means 'the dead ones,' or maybe just 'the dead.'"

"Or maybe 'dead men,'" Rhodes said.

"Why the Spanish name?" Hack asked.

"Nobody knows," Rhodes said. "There aren't many Chicano members of the gang, as far as I know. Besides, they started a long time ago. It could be that someone just liked the sound of it."

"Anyway you slice it, they're bad business," Lawton said.

"You know it," Hack said. "I surely do wish you hadn't been askin' me to check up on whether the DPS boys had seen any motorsickles in the county lately, Sheriff. Even just thinkin' that Los Muertos might be tied into somethin' that you're workin' on makes me a little nervous."

"You reckon all them stories they tell on that bunch are true?" Lawton asked.

"I don't know," Hack said, "but if even half of 'em are, then I don't want a thing to do with those boys."

"To tell the truth, I don't either," Rhodes said. He leaned forward in the chair. There was a high-pitched squeak.

"We got to get us some WD-40," Hack said.

Just then there was an alarming crashing and clattering from the air conditioner. It sounded as if someone had thrown a pair of pliers into the fan motor. The sound increased in intensity and pitch, then gradually began to trail off until it sounded more like someone tapping on a piece of steel with a ball-peen hammer. Then there was no noise at all. The air conditioner had stopped completely.

"I told you so," Hack said.

6

MOST OF WHAT Rhodes knew about Los Muertos, he'd read in the newspapers or heard from other members of the law-enforcement fraternity. None of it was good. For the more than twenty-five years of the gang's existence, the members of its various chapters had been more or less at war with the members of any other gangs in the state, as well as among themselves. There had been numerous crimes linked to the gang, and some of them had even been proved and tried in court. Rhodes could recall at least two convictions for armed robbery and one for murder. There were probably plenty of minor convictions for assault that he'd never heard of.

Lately, however, the members of various chapters had settled their differences, formed a rough confederation, and begun making money the new-fashioned way—running dope. Their bikes were fast and easily maneuverable over most terrain. Most of them could travel wherever and whenever they wanted, not being too tied to regular jobs, homes, and families. They were a close-knit group and trusted no one, as most of their secrets stayed within the gang.

No one knew exactly where the dope—mostly marijuana—came from. One theory was that it was grown in Mexico and then smuggled across the border, but Rhodes and many others tended to discount that theory on the grounds that it would involve trusting third, or maybe even fourth, parties, unless Los Muertos crossed the border themselves. Someone would have had to grow the weed, and someone would have had to bring it across. Rhodes didn't know where they got the dope, but he didn't think it came from Mexico.

Blacklin County didn't have a dope problem. Or at least it didn't have a dope problem that Rhodes knew about. It was true that every now and then one of the deputies would come in with a high-school kid who had a little marijuana in a baggie. Usually it was hardly enough to measure. Rhodes doubted that he'd seen anywhere near a pound of marijuana in his whole tenure as sheriff, taking it all together. Maybe he was letting his imagination get the better of him. All because of a little tattoo.

He left Hack and Lawton looking disconsolately at the air conditioner and went out into the late afternoon heat. Soon the inside of the office would be like the inside of a baked potato. He hoped they could get the air conditioner repaired soon. He'd left Hack instructions to call Romig's Appliance first thing in the morning.

He idly laid his hand on top of the white county car, then jerked it back. The roof had been baking in the afternoon sun and was as hot as an exhaust pipe after the Indy 500.

Then he remembered that he hadn't eaten lunch. He went back inside and called Ivy Daniel, who agreed to go out for a bite with him. He left again, but this time Hack and Lawton were smirking wisely at one another, forgetting the air conditioner for the moment.

Rhodes wished that he could clarify his thoughts about Ivy. He guessed that in the way of small towns everywhere, it was pretty general knowledge that they were "keeping company" and that they were being closely watched for signs of impending matrimony.

He wasn't sure that he was ready to let the town rumor him into marriage, however, and he really had no idea how Ivy felt about the subject. It wasn't something that they had talked about.

When Rhodes's wife had died, he'd felt an emptiness that he thought would never go away. It had, very slowly, and one of the reasons was Ivy Daniel. He'd begun to feel very strongly for her, and in fact he told himself that that was part of the problem. He never wanted to lose someone and feel that emptiness again. If he got too attached to Ivy, he would be vulnerable.

Ivy, on the other hand, was independently minded. Rhodes told himself that she was quite happy to be going out with him occasionally to eat or visiting at his house when there was time. He told himself that she wouldn't be happy as his wife—he kept terrible hours, he was on call all day, every day, he never knew when he'd be at home. He also knew what rationalization was.

He picked Ivy up at her house. She was dressed in jeans and a white blouse, and Rhodes realized again how slim and youthful she looked. He tried to suck in his stomach so that his belt buckle would show.

"Where are we going to eat?" Ivy asked as she got in the car.

"Lester's," Rhodes said.

"Great," Ivy said. "I haven't been to Lester's in a week or two, and that's too long."

Lester's was just on the outskirts of Clearview. It was not fancy enough to be called a restaurant, or even a cafe. Lester's was a barbecue joint, and it looked the part.

When Rhodes and Ivy drove up there were three cars and a pickup parked in front of what looked like an old house in poor repair. It had once been painted green, but that had been years ago. It had a slight list to the left, as if someone very large had given it a shove. In front was a piece of plywood on which someone had printed in black paint, with a very wide brush and an unsteady hand: LESTERS BBQ. As Hack had once told Rhodes, "Lester don't believe in puttin' up a front."

Ivy and Rhodes walked across the dry grass of the yard to the front door. They stepped up on a wooden step and went inside. The inside of Lester's was dim and permeated by the smell of barbecue. They found an empty table and sat in two rickety chairs.

There was no cloth on the table, which was covered by a worn but spotless piece of linoleum. The menu was hand-printed on a piece of plain white paper. There wasn't much choice. You could have barbecue with beans or without beans. White bread. Water, tea, or a soft drink.

Lester waited on the tables himself, and he came in shortly after Rhodes and Ivy were seated. He was an old, wrinkled black man, with skin so smooth it looked like polished wood. He'd been making and selling barbecue since Rhodes was a boy.

"How you, Mist' Rhodes?" Lester asked in his deep, husky voice. "An' you, Miss Ivy?"

"We're fine, Lester," Rhodes said. "How's the meat today?"

"Nice an' lean, Mist' Rhodes," Lester said. "Hard to find a nice lean brisket these days, but I do it."

"We'll both have a plate with beans, then," Rhodes said. "And I'll have a Dr. Pepper."

"Me, too," Ivy said. "I'm picking up your bad habits."

"Man ain't got no bad habits," Lester said. He went back into the kitchen to slice the meat. He had a one-man operation and intended to keep it that way.

"What's new?" Ivy said.

Rhodes told her about the conversation with Dr. Rawlings and about Bert Ramsey. It sometimes surprised him how easily he could talk to her.

"Bert Ramsey built the fence around my backyard," Ivy said. "About five years ago. He seemed like a nice, hardworking sort of a man. Why would anybody kill him?"

Rhodes told her about the Los Muertos tattoo, and about Ramsey's mother hearing the motorcycles. He went on to tell her about Buster Cullens and Wyneva.

"And you don't think there's any connection between Bert's murder and those boxes he found?"

"There doesn't seem to be," Rhodes said. "No one involved in that had any reason to kill Bert. As far as I know, nothing illegal has been done. Adams and Rawlings seemed pretty cooperative."

"Then all you have there is a mess."

"Right. Somehow, some way, we've got to get those things taken care of."

They talked quietly, unaware of the other occupants of the room, all of whom were concentrating on their food. The only real sounds were the clicking of silverware against the heavy china plates that Lester provided.

Then Lester arrived with their food. The meat was cooked just the way Rhodes liked it, slowly, all day, over a hickory fire. Lester had not yet given in to the latest fad, that of cooking his barbecue over mesquite wood.

But it was the sauce that Rhodes liked best, and the sauce was Lester's greatest secret. Not too thick, not too thin, it was a dark, reddish-black in color, spiced just right by whatever secret ingredients Lester cooked into it. It had a bite, but not too much of one. It was slightly sweet, but tantalizingly so. Rhodes loved to dip his bread in it and eat it, with hardly a guilty thought of his waistline. Ivy didn't mind. She liked it, too. When they finished, their plates were gleaming white.

"Lester won't even have to wash those if he doesn't want to," Rhodes said, though he knew Lester would. The county health inspector had told Rhodes that Lester had the cleanest kitchen in the territory.

Rhodes paid Lester, who had an ancient cash register on a table near the door. A collector would have paid a premium price for that cash register, Rhodes thought.

It was only seven-thirty when they stepped outside, which meant that there was plenty of daylight left. "I thought I'd ride out to Mrs. Ramsey's," Rhodes said. "I've got to find out about that tattoo. You want to come along?"

"Sure," Ivy said. "I never pass up a chance to see how the law operates." She took his arm and they walked to the car.

Mrs. Ramsey's house, like Bert's, looked well kept up. Rhodes suspected that Bert was probably responsible, since Mrs. Ramsey hardly looked the type to favor yard work. The house had been recently painted, and the screens of the neat screened-in porch on the front looked almost new. There were no tears in them anywhere. Mrs. Ramsey's old Ford sat beside the house in the dirt driveway.

"You don't have to go in," Rhodes said as he stopped the car. It always made him a little uncomfortable to interrogate women, for some reason. Not that he wasn't good at it. It was just a feeling that he got, and he wasn't sure how Ivy would feel about the situation.

"Don't be silly," Ivy said. "I'm not going to sit out here in this hot car. Besides, I might be able to help. The poor woman must feel terrible about what's happened."

"Thanks," Rhodes said. He was glad that Ivy would be coming in. Just having her there might make things easier. They got out of the car and walked to the porch. Rhodes rapped with his knuckles on the wooden frame of the screen door, causing it to rattle loosely.

They heard Mrs. Ramsey's voice from inside. "Comin'."

Rhodes watched through the screen as she came into view from the front room. Her step was heavy, and he almost expected to hear the floorboards groan under her weight. She lifted the hook latch from the screen and held it open. "Y'all come on in," she said.

Mrs. Ramsey's living room was not as neat as her son's. A yellow Afghan on the back of the couch was in disarray, and the plant on the television set obviously hadn't been watered in far too long. The straight-backed wooden chairs were old and worn. The television set, however, was nearly brand new.

Mrs. Ramsey saw Rhodes looking at the television. "Bert bought me that," she said. "He bought me lots of things." She looked around, as if trying to see what else her son had bought her. Then she looked back at Rhodes.

"Mrs. Ramsey, this is Ivy Daniel," Rhodes said. "She's a friend of mine."

"Pleased to meet you," Mrs. Ramsey said. "Y'all have a seat."

Rhodes and Ivy sat in the wooden chairs. Mrs. Ramsey sank to the couch. The room was dim and cool. Rhodes was aware of an efficient window-unit air conditioner purring quietly, and he thought of Hack and Lawton down at the jail.

"I know this is a bad time, Mrs. Ramsey," Rhodes began, "but I have to ask you a few questions." He paused and looked at Mrs. Ramsey, who sat solidly and quietly on the couch.

The silence stretched out. Rhodes looked at Ivy, who shrugged. Rhodes decided to go ahead.

"Mrs. Ramsey, I always thought that Bert was in the army before he came back here to work, but what you said last night about the motorcycles made me wonder. Was Bert ever a member of one of those motorcycle gangs?"

Mrs. Ramsey didn't move. Rhodes waited. Finally, she said, "I heard motorsickles last night. Buster Cullens has a motorsickle."

"I know," Rhodes said. "I've seen it. But what I'm asking about is Bert, not Buster Cullens."

"Bert was livin' in sin with that Wyneva before Buster Cullens come up here. Bert was a good boy, before he got mixed up with them motorsickles."

"That's what I'd like to know about," Rhodes said. "The motorcycles."

"That was a long time ago," Mrs. Ramsey said.

"How long?" Ivy asked. Rhodes was surprised, but he didn't say anything. He figured Ivy knew what she was doing.

Mrs. Ramsey's eyes had a sad, faraway look. "It was right after he got out of high school," she said. "His pa had died the year before, and Bert took it pretty good. We lived right in this house, here. I've got a picture of Bert in his graduation gown. He was standing right by that chair you're sittin' in. It was that summer he got mixed up with a bad crowd, drinkin', ridin' them motorsickles. It wasn't that he did anything real wrong. That was later, with that Wyneva."

"He had a tattoo," Rhodes said.

"He got that tattoo that summer," Mrs. Ramsey said. "He said he was one of the dead, now. I didn't know what he meant, but I thought maybe his daddy dyin' affected him more than he let on. But he got over it, finally, come back here, settled down, and made somethin' of himself. But that Wyneva was the ruination of him. And then them motorsickles come back. . . ."

"When?" Ivy asked. "When did the motorcycles come back?"

"Two years ago," Mrs. Ramsey said.

Rhodes looked at her, surprised. He wasn't able to keep tabs on every single thing in Blacklin County, but he didn't think that a gang of motorcyclists like Los Muertos could hide out there for two years without him hearing a thing about it. "Are you sure?" he asked.

"About that," Mrs. Ramsey said. "It was after he took up with that Wyneva, but a good while before they started in to livin' in sin."

"Did you ever see them?" Rhodes asked.

"No, but then they never came around very often. I'd hear 'em in the night, though. Late. They always woke me up." Mrs. Ramsey shifted her weight on the couch.

Ivy stood up. "Thank you, Mrs. Ramsey," she said. "I believe it's time for us to go."

Rhodes stood up with her. "Yes," he said. "I appreciate your time, Mrs. Ramsey. I may have to talk with you again." Mrs. Ramsey started to rise from the couch. "Don't you get up. We can see ourselves to the door."

When they were in the car, Rhodes said, "I ought to swear you in. You'd make a good deputy."

Ivy smiled. "Probably not. She just needed someone she felt comfortable with. You're too intimidating."

Rhodes had to laugh at that. He considered himself one of the least intimidating men he knew, even though he wore a badge.

Ivy shook her head. "No," she said, "don't laugh. It's true. I know you don't threaten or bully, but you look so *serious.*"

"I am serious," Rhodes told her. "Murder is serious. I don't like it."

"I know," Ivy said. "That's one of the things I like about you."

It had gotten dark while they were in the house with Mrs. Ramsey, and Rhodes hoped that Ivy couldn't see him blushing.

7

As THEY DROVE slowly down the back roads on the way to town, Rhodes remembered summer nights as a child, riding in the car with his family. There hadn't been any television sets then, and often his father would drive them around in the family car, touring the dark and peaceful country. The country still looked peaceful, despite the death of Bert Ramsey, but it was no longer dark. Every house and yard and most of the barns were bathed in the eerie blue glow of a mercury vapor lamp.

Rhodes stopped the car in Bert Ramsey's front yard. "I just want to see what it must have been like," he told Ivy. "Whoever shot him was in plain sight of the road, what with that lamp lighting everything up. If anybody came by, they would have seen. Somebody took a big chance."

"Not too many people come by here," Ivy said. "I'll bet we could sit here for hours and not see more than one car go by."

Something in her voice made Rhodes turn and look at her. Her face looked a little strange and unearthly in the blue light, but suddenly Rhodes felt like a teenager, or at least as much like a teenager as a middle-aged man could feel. Here he was, parked in the country, on a lonely stretch of road, with a woman beside him in the car. For an instant, or the briefest part of an instant, he remembered other summer nights and other cars, not the ones his father drove, but the ones he drove. He remembered the girls who had ridden in those cars with him, and he felt a tightening in the back of his throat and in the pit of his stomach.

He put his right arm up on the seat back, and Ivy slid into the curve that it made. They looked at each other, and when he kissed her he knew that he was in real trouble this time.

Dr. Malcolm Rawlings didn't look very much like a doctor to Rhodes. He had on a polo shirt with an alligator where the pocket should be, but there was no pocket. A cigarette package caused the doctor an obvious problem, because he was carrying it in his left hand. He had on a pair of old blue slacks, held up with a brown belt, and a pair of brown loafers. He had thinning, reddish-brown hair and the build of a former athlete, maybe a baseball player.

He stood looking around the jail office and then shook a cigarette out of his package. Jamming the package in the left front pocket of his slacks, he brought a disposable lighter from the right pocket and lit the cigarette. Then he walked over and shook hands with Rhodes.

"I'm Dr. Malcolm Rawlings," he said. "You must be Sheriff Rhodes."

"That's right," Rhodes said. "This is Hack Jensen."

Hack walked over from the radio table and shook hands.

Rawlings took a deep drag from his cigarette and puffed the white smoke into the air. Its odor seemed particularly sharp to Rhodes, since neither he nor Hack smoked.

Rawlings pulled a worn billfold from his back pocket, opened it, and took out a folded piece of paper. "Here's that list you asked for, Sheriff. That ought to take care of everything." He stood waiting, as if ready for Rhodes to tell him to leave.

"Fine, Dr. Rawlings," Rhodes said. "Come on over

here and have a seat." Rhodes walked to his desk and sat in his chair. There was a captain's chair by the desk. Rawlings sat in it reluctantly.

"What's that hole over there?" Rawlings asked suddenly, looking at the opposite wall.

"That's where the air conditioner used to be," Hack said. "Kinda warm in here, ain't it?"

Rawlings didn't answer. He turned back to Rhodes. "I'm in kind of a rush, Sheriff," he said. "I have to get back and—"

"Just a minute," Rhodes said. "You don't seem to realize the problem here. I called the state Health Department about an hour ago, and I was told that I'd have to sue you if I wanted to get you to take care of what you've dumped in my county. And I was told that I'd probably lose the suit unless I could definitely prove that you'd caused a health problem, which I probably can't prove. So, I'm a little frustrated. On top of that there's been a murder. And you think you need to leave in a hurry?"

Rawlings looked around for an ashtray. Not finding one in sight, he moved his fingers to the cigarette's filter tip. "Uh, well, I just thought that, ah . . ."

"You just thought you'd leave me stuck with the problem, I guess," Rhodes said. "But it won't work like that. You're not going anywhere until we both go over to the funeral home and check that list against the remains in the boxes. And then we're going to decide what to do with them."

"Can you force me to do that?" Rawlings asked. "I mean, is it legal?"

"I'm not sure," Rhodes said. "Shall we call the county judge and get a ruling?"

"No, no, of course not," Rawlings said. "That won't be necessary at all. I'll be glad to go with you."

"Fine," Rhodes said. "Let's go. You can ride with me."

Rawlings didn't look happy, but he went.

Clyde Ballinger watched as Rawlings and Rhodes inventoried the contents of the boxes. "Tell you what, Doctor," Ballinger said, "as one professional man to another, I can't see how you could do such a thing as to dump those body parts like that. Seems like you could get in real trouble with your professional organizations. I know if I were to try it, why I'd be branded forever."

Rawlings looked up. "I've explained the circumstances," he said. "There's not going to be any report of this, is there?"

"Not if everything tallies and we can arrange a satisfactory way to dispose of these things," Rhodes said. He didn't really have any desire to ruin Rawlings's reputation.

"I don't know," Ballinger said. "It just doesn't seem right. I bet Carella or the boys at the 87th wouldn't let something like this slide by."

It was Rhodes's turn to look at him. "Seems to me you could be a little more helpful, yourself, Clyde," he said. "You don't seem to want to do a thing about this."

"And get sued? You must be kidding. I wouldn't touch this for a million bucks. Not without a court order. The way I see it, it's the doctor's problem."

"I did nothing illegal," Rawlings said.

"Just immoral," Ballinger said.

"Cut it out," Rhodes told them. "Let us finish checking, Clyde."

It was a fairly gruesome business, going through the three boxes, and Rhodes wasn't too happy to be doing it. However, it was necessary, and he kept going along, matching the limbs up to the list that Rawlings had brought, watching the doctor as he made a neat little check mark whenever there was a match. Soon they were all done.

"Everything accounted for," Rawlings said. "Let's get out of here." He had goose bumps on his arms from the chill of the room. "I need a cigarette."

"We're not going anywhere," Rhodes said. "Not until we settle the question of what's to be done with all this." He gestured at the boxes and the neatly wrapped limbs scattered around.

"That's all between you two," Ballinger said. "I'm not going to have a thing to do with it."

"All right, all right," Rawlings said. "Let's get to a phone, and I'll see what I can do."

They left the room and went outside. Ballinger took them to his office. Rawlings had lit a cigarette, but Ballinger made him put it out. "I don't want my books smoked up," he said.

Rawlings paid no attention to Ballinger's books once they were in the office. He went right for the phone and punched long distance information. When he got a voice on the other end, he asked for the number of Gulfside Biomedical Waste Disposal. He hung up, then dialed the number using his calling-card digits. His conversation was not satisfactory.

"They won't take these items," he said. "They'll take any that I have in the future, but not these. I shouldn't have told them the whole story."

Rhodes looked at Ballinger.

Ballinger looked at Rawlings.

"Look," Rawlings said, an edge in his voice, "I was just trying to save a buck." He reached in his pants pocket for his mangled cigarette pack, looked at Ballinger, and withdrew his hand. "They just didn't mean anything to me, is all. I just used them for tissue samples. It was like they were something I bought at the dime store. Didn't you ever get to feeling that way about the bodies you deal with?"

Ballinger managed a shocked look. "We here at Ballinger's take a personal pride and care with every client. It's very important to us that the loved ones are treated with respect and dignity. We would never, ever—"

"Skip it," Rawlings said. "I wasn't interested in a sales pitch."

"What about it, Clyde?" Rhodes asked.

"Well, I might be persuaded," Ballinger said.

"Wait a minute," Rawlings said. "Persuaded to what?"

"To bury your leavings," Ballinger said. "To get your ass out of the crack you got it into."

"How much?" Rawlings asked.

Ballinger told him.

"But . . . but that's more than it would have cost me to get them burned at the biomedical place. That's robbery!"

"Not exactly," Rhodes said. "It's just taking advantage of a situation, which may not be exactly fair, but then nobody asked you to dump things in this county."

Rawlings thought about it for a minute. "No charges will be filed if I get this taken care of? No publicity?"

"People talk in a little town like this," Rhodes said. "I can't make any promises. But there won't be anything done in court."

Rawlings reached into his back pocket and pulled out a worn leather billfold, cracked and ripped in places, but stuffed full. "Will cash be OK?"

There was a new air conditioner in the hole in the wall. Hack and Lawton were smiling in contentment.

"Listen how quiet that sucker is," Hack said.

"Sure enough," Lawton said. "And cool, too."

"Too cool for some folks, I guess," Hack said.

"Maybe too cool for us," Rhodes said, "especially when the commissioners get the bill." Robert Romig had been in early that morning and looked over the old unit. He'd told Rhodes that there wasn't a chance of fixing it, and the sheriff had ordered a new one. He hoped the county had the money in the budget.

"Wasn't talkin' about us," Hack said.

Rhodes knew then that he'd missed a hint. Something had happened while he was at Ballinger's.

"Who's it too cool for?" he asked.

"Somebody who'd steal a gas stove," Hack said.

"A gas stove? To cook on?" Rhodes wasn't quite sure what was being discussed, but then he often felt that way when Hack was reporting a crime.

"Not that kind," Lawton said helpfully. Hack glared at him.

"A Dearborn heater," Hack said. "One of those that you can back up to in the winter. Nothing feels better when it's cold than being able to back up to a heater like that."

"It has a cool top," Lawton said. "You can put your hand on the top, or set a flowerpot on it, or anything."

"I know," Rhodes said. "I have that kind of heater at my house."

"When's the last time you checked?" Hack asked.

"You mean to tell me somebody stole my stove?" Rhodes said.

"Maybe not," Hack said, "but don't be too sure. Somebody stole two of 'em out of Ham Richardson's rent house over on Rose Street. The renters skipped out two weeks ago, and they took everything they could, even the light bulbs, but they left the stoves."

"I remember that," Rhodes said. "Maybe they came back for the stoves when they got moved in somewhere else."

"That's what I think," Lawton said. "Some don't agree, though."

Hack shook his head. "It could be," he said. "Ru—the new deputy is checkin' out the scene."

"Let me know if she finds out anything," Rhodes said. "I'm going home and have a sandwich. You all having something brought in?"

"Lawton's goin' for hamburgers," Hack said. "When you comin' back in?"

"Later," Rhodes said.

Rhodes would never have admitted it, but he liked to go home for lunch, not because he liked bologna sandwiches, which was about all he ever ate there, but because he could catch all or part of the *Million Dollar Movie* for the day. Kathy had kept after him about eating a more balanced diet, but she'd never bothered him about the movie. He wouldn't have missed her very much if she had.

The feature was *The Naked Jungle,* which he'd seen several times before—a good thing, since he'd missed the first twenty minutes. With any luck, though, he'd get to see the climactic scenes with the attacking army ants devouring everything in their path. Besides, he'd always liked Eleanor Parker, if not the usually wooden Charlton Heston.

As he ate the sandwich and watched the movie, Rhodes worried about the death of Bert Ramsey. He'd thought from the beginning, or at least since Ruth Grady had discovered the yellow tags, that Ramsey's death had nothing to do with the arms and legs he'd found. It had to be something else. Ramsey's conspicuous consumption, not to mention the cash in the dresser drawer (now safely locked in the jail safe), pointed to something, and possibly something illegal. The Los Muertos connection gave a pretty good hint that dope was involved. But how?

Rhodes didn't like the idea that there was something going on in the county without his being aware of it. Of course, Los Muertos didn't have to be staying there. They could be riding in and out, which would be easy enough to do without anyone's being conscious of their presence. Late at night on any of the little-traveled back roads, they could come and go with impunity. A deputy would see them only on an off chance.

Then there were Buster Cullens and Wyneva. He had only Mrs. Ramsey's accusation to go on there. The fact that Cullens was living with Bert's old girl friend and that he rode a motorcycle wouldn't go far toward convicting him. Wouldn't even come close to being grounds for arrest, for that matter. Still, it was worth considering.

What he needed was more and better information; he needed someone who had heard something. It was time to start talking to the informants. You couldn't have as much cash on hand as Bert Ramsey had and not cause some talk, not in Blacklin County, you couldn't. There was bound to be someone out there who'd heard something, no matter how insignificant.

The shotgun bothered Rhodes, too. A shotgun wasn't something you carried around on a motorcycle, right out in the open. A cyclist would maybe carry a pistol, or a knife. Maybe even a length of chain around his waist. But a shotgun? No way. Unless, of course, he carried it cowboy style, in a leather scabbard. Rhodes supposed it could be concealed on a motorcycle easily enough that way.

He had another sandwich, drank a canned Dr. Pepper, even though he vastly preferred the bottled ones, and watched the end of the movie. Then he went into the bedroom and got ten one-dollar bills out of a cigar box he kept on top of the dresser. He was willing to pay for information, but he wasn't going to pay much.

The cigar box had once held Hav-A-Tampa Jewel cigars. Rhodes had been to a restaurant where the waiter brought all the male diners a Hav-A-Tampa Jewel after dinner. He remembered that the cigars were small, with a wooden tip. He wondered if they were still being made. As he closed the lid of the box, the telephone rang.

8

HACK WAS ON the line. "I've had a call about some motorsickles, Sheriff," he said.

Rhodes had a feeling he'd just saved a few dollars.

"You want to check it out yourself, or have somebody else do it?" Hack asked.

"I'll check it," Rhodes said. "Who made the call?"

"You sure you don't want me to put Ruth on this one?" Hack asked. Rhodes noticed that he hadn't called her "the new deputy," and he wondered what was going on.

"No," Rhodes said. "I want to take care of this myself. Now, who made the call?"

Hack didn't exactly laugh. "Mrs. Wilkie," he said.

"Oh," Rhodes said. After a few seconds, he said, "I'll take care of it anyway. I'll be going out there now."

"All right, Sheriff," Hack said. "You're the boss." He hung up.

Rhodes held the phone for a minute, then set it down. He walked back to the dresser, opened the cigar box, and put the ten dollars back inside. He thought that he'd rather have paid out the money than visit Mrs. Wilkie, but there wasn't really any choice.

It wasn't that he exactly disliked Mrs. Wilkie; it was just that she had ideas that he didn't agree with. One of the main ones was that he should marry her. His wife had been dead about a year when Mrs. Wilkie began making what Rhodes considered "advances." She was at least ten years older than he, though she would never have admitted it, and she had a good ten pounds on him. She also had the most amazing red hair he'd ever seen, or to put it more accurately, the most amazing *orange* hair he'd ever seen. After Rhodes had become involved with Ivy, Mrs. Wilkie had more or less given up her pursuit, but the thought of having to meet with her made him slightly nervous. It wasn't beyond her to have concocted some story just to get him out to Milsby, the tiny community where she lived. No wonder Hack had been nearly laughing.

Still, it didn't seem likely that Mrs. Wilkie would have made up a story about motorcycles. Hardly anyone knew that Rhodes was looking for that sort of information. He'd have to check it out.

Rhodes drove by the old schoolhouse which was just about all that remained of what had once been the town of Milsby. He was fond of that schoolhouse, because that was where he'd first really become aware of Ivy Daniel.

He hadn't really allowed himself to think of Ivy all day. After last night, he was sure that they had crossed a certain line in their relationship and that there would be no going back to where they had been before. He was going to have to give that some serious thought, but not until he had time to devote his full energy to it.

Mrs. Wilkie lived in a nondescript brick-veneer house that was a little newer than most of the homes around it. Not too many houses had been built in Milsby in the last few years.

Rhodes parked in the drive, got out, and knocked on the door.

Mrs. Wilkie was a little flustered to see him. "Oh, my," she said. "I really didn't expect . . . I mean, I thought one of the deputies . . ."

"I do a lot of the work myself," Rhodes said. "We're a pretty small county." He smiled.

"Well, come in, come in," Mrs. Wilkie said, opening the door wider.

Rhodes stepped inside. Mrs. Wilkie was wearing a flowered print dress of the same basic color as her hair, with bright yellow and white flowers on it. The yellow flowers had white centers; the white ones had yellow centers. It was quite a sight.

The living room in which they stood didn't go with the house. It reminded Rhodes of something you might have seen fifty years before. On his left was a bookcase covered with a heavy black stain. It had glass doors that slid up to the top and protected a very old, green *World Book Encyclopedia* and a complete set of *The Book of Knowledge*. There was a set of the works of Mark Twain, and a set of the complete works of James Whitcomb Riley. The couch and chairs all had print covers, and there were doilies on the arms. Even the television set was old. It had a round picture tube.

"Sit down, Sheriff," Mrs. Wilkie said.

Rhodes sat in one of the chairs. Its springs had held up well over the years. "I understand that you've had some trouble with motorcycles," he said.

Mrs. Wilkie put her hand to her hair and patted it. "That's right, Sheriff. It's just disgraceful, the noise they make. And all hours of the night."

"They come by the house, here?"

"Yes, right in front, rousing the whole neighborhood. Al James lives right down the road, and she says—"

Rhodes interrupted. "Have they ever come by during the day?"

"No, never, but Al says—"

"Has anybody seen who these motorcycle riders are?"

"Please, Sheriff, I'm trying to tell you something." Mrs. Wilkie sounded exasperated, and Rhodes didn't blame her. He'd been breaking in and not letting her tell her story the way she wanted. He knew better, but he was always defensive around her, and he was trying to get the information and get out as quickly as possible. He didn't let things affect him that way, usually.

"I'm sorry," Rhodes said. "What about Mrs. James?"

"Well, as I was trying to say, Al believes that they're camping out down by the lake on the Gottschalk place. She hasn't seen them, and as far as I know no one else has seen them. They don't seem to be around during the day. But we hear them every night, and Al says they come up that road that runs by her house and on down by the Gottschalk land. So she thinks that's where they are."

"How long has this been going on?" Rhodes asked.

"Not long, I can assure you, or I would have called before now," Mrs. Wilkie said. Her tone made it clear that she had suffered great aggravation. "I value my rest, Sheriff, and when I'm disturbed in the middle of the night I can seldom get back to sleep. The first time I heard them was last Thursday."

And Bert Ramsey gets himself killed on Saturday night, Rhodes thought, after his mother hears motorcyles. "I think I'd better get on down to that lake," he said. "I'll see if anyone's there, and I'll find out if they have permission to be there. If they don't, I'll move them along and maybe you can begin getting a little rest again."

"Oh, good," Mrs. Wilkie said. "You just don't know what it's like to be disturbed like that."

Rhodes wondered how many nights in the last year he'd been disturbed by telephone calls from people wanting him to locate wayward tomcats or quiet down noisy parties or settle a marital argument. Probably a lot more often than Mrs. Wilkie had. But he didn't say anything. He got up to leave.

Mrs. Wilkie stepped to his side and plucked at his

sleeve. "You don't really need to rush off," she said coyly. "Wouldn't you like a cup of coffee? I could perk some in just a minute."

Rhodes, who didn't drink coffee under any circumstances, felt depressed. He'd thought Mrs. Wilkie had given up on him, but evidently she hadn't, quite. Probably since his relationship with Ivy Daniel hadn't developed beyond the "good friends" stage, at least in its most public phase, Mrs. Wilkie was encouraged.

"Ah, no," he said. "It's getting late, and I'd like to get on down there before it gets dark."

It was a good long time until dark, and Mrs. Wilkie knew it. Rhodes had to give her credit, though. She let him go with good grace. As he backed out of the drive, he saw her standing in the door in her flamboyant print dress.

It was still hot and dry, and a rooster-tail of white dust followed the county car along the dirt road onto which Rhodes turned at Al James's house. The cows had grazed nearly all the grass off the pastures beside the road, and Rhodes could see bare dirt and rock showing through. The cows were gathered under the trees to take advantage of the little relief offered by the shade. If it didn't rain, and rain soon, the cattlemen would be in real trouble.

Rhodes came to the Gottschalk property and turned in. There was no gate, only a cattle guard of iron pipe. Rhodes had never thought cattle guards were very effective, and he was pretty sure Gottschalk wasn't running any cows on his land. Otherwise, there would have been a gate.

The car topped a gentle rise, following the ruts that made up what now passed for a road, and Rhodes looked down at the lake. It really wasn't a lake, of course, and probably wouldn't have been considered much more than a good-sized swimming hole in a wetter part of the country, but in Texas it passed for a lake. Unfortunately, because of the hot, dry weather, the lake was even smaller than usual. About half of the shallow end was now mostly mud-flat, and most of the water was concentrated by the twelve-foot-high dam. Also near the dam, but a good way out on the dry land, there were four motorcycles and a small tent. There was a huge oak tree nearby, and four men sat under it. Rhodes drove on down.

The four men didn't bother to get up when Rhodes stopped the car and stepped out. They just looked at him. He looked back. All four were wearing jeans covered with dirt and grease, and all had on denim vests but no shirts. Rhodes was surprised that all of them looked fairly clean. He guessed that they'd been swimming in the lake to keep cool.

Finally, one of them spoke. He was sitting with his back against the trunk of the tree, smoking a cigarette. "Well, fellas, looks like we've got us a visit from the High Sheriff himself. What's the trouble, Sheriff?"

Rhodes looked at the man. He was older than Rhodes would have thought, and he didn't really fit Rhodes's idea of a biker at all. His iron-colored hair was greasy, but it was short and combed straight back in a widow's peak. He looked quite short, and Rhodes guessed that if he stood up he wouldn't be over five-feet five or six. He was slightly pudgy, but his face had a vaguely satanic look because of a pointed chin. He looked to Rhodes like a congenital liar. On one arm was the Los Muertos tattoo.

"I was just wondering if you folks had permission to camp here," Rhodes said. His eyes looked over the area, but no shotgun was in sight. It could have been in the tent, however.

"Well, now, Sheriff," the one who had spoken first said, "I expect we have as much right to be here as you do. More, in fact. Isn't that right, Nellie?"

The man addressed as Nellie stood up. His hair was

cropped close to his head, and he looked lean and fit. In fact, Rhodes thought he looked a lot like the German SS officers in old war movies. "That's right, Rapper." He looked at Rhodes. "The guy that owns this land is my uncle. He said it was fine with him if we stayed here a few days. Don't recall him saying anything about letting anyone else visit, though."

"I'm investigating a complaint," Rhodes said.

Rapper stood up. Rhodes had been right about his height. "What complaint would that be, Sheriff?"

"Some of the residents have mentioned a lot of noise late at night," Rhodes said.

"That's just too bad," Rapper said. "We have a right to go where we please, when we please. If the local yokels don't like it, they can buy some ear plugs."

One of the other men stood up. He had wavy hair that seemed to Rhodes to have a strangely greenish tinge. "Yuh," he said. "You tell 'em, Rapper. If they don't like it, let 'em—"

"Shut up, Jayse," Rapper said. He didn't even bother to look at the man, who shut up immediately. Rhodes didn't have any doubt who was the boss of this bunch. He wondered if it was another case of the little guy who loved and took advantage of authority.

"Let me tell you something, Sheriff," Rapper said. "We're just four guys who like the great outdoors. We may drive noisy machines, but we're not hurting anybody. So why don't you just go catch some real criminals and leave us alone. If you do, we won't report you for trespassing."

The arrogance seemed to come off the little man in waves, and Rhodes could sense that he was accustomed to getting his way through fear and intimidation. Rhodes, however, didn't intimidate as easily as some people might have guessed by looking at his easy-going face. "I'll leave," he said. "But if I have any more complaints about the noise, I'll have a deputy out on these roads every night. With backup from the DPS. And if one of you has a cracked taillight or goes one mile an hour over the speed limit, you'll be looking at the inside of a cell. We'll check your records, too, and if there're any outstanding warrants against you, you'll be a gone goose."

"Yuh, uh, don't talk to Rapper like that, man," Jayse said. "He's put guys—"

"Shut up, asshole," Rapper said, again without even looking at Jayse.

"Ah, but Rapper . . ." Jayse began.

Rapper spun on him. "I said shut up!" he screamed. His face turned a deep, dark red as the blood rushed to it. The loose skin under his neck shook like a turkey's wattle.

Jayse cowered away. Nellie said nothing. The fourth man still hadn't moved.

Rapper controlled himself with a visible effort and turned back to Rhodes. "We'll be good little boys, Sheriff. You can tell the widows and orphans that they can sleep well tonight. We'll tippytoe down the roads from now on." His voice dripped with sarcasm.

Rhodes accepted the meaning and not the intent. "Fine. I'm sure you're as good as your word. Enjoy your camping trip." He walked to his car and got in. As he drove away, he could see Rapper starting for Jayse with balled fists. The fourth man still hadn't moved. Nellie was watching calmly.

9

RHODES BELIEVED THAT he was pretty good at reading people, and he read Rapper as a sadistic bully, just exactly the type who might blow away a man with a shotgun, even if the man was standing in his own front door. The fact that Rhodes hadn't seen a shotgun didn't mean much. If he'd tried to look into the tent, Rapper would no doubt have caused trouble.

It bothered Rhodes that Rapper had agreed so readily to keep down the noise. Despite his sarcasm, Rapper had meant what he said, or so Rhodes believed. Rapper wouldn't have given in so easily on that point under ordinary circumstances. Which probably meant that he had something else to hide, something that he didn't want to jeopardize because of petty hassles. Murder was something to hide, all right.

As the car's tires rapped across the cattle guard, the radio crackled and Hack came on. Hack didn't believe much in radio discipline. "You out there, Sheriff?" he asked.

Rhodes picked up the mike. "I'm here. What's up?"

"Thought you might want to come on by the jail when you get a chance. The new deputy's here, and she has somethin' to tell you." They were back to "the new deputy," Rhodes thought. At least when Ruth was around. "Clyde Ballinger called, too. Says to tell you that Bert Ramsey's funeral will be tomorrow at ten o'clock, in the funeral chapel."

"Got it. That all?" Rhodes said.

"There's a couple of other little things," Hack said. "They'll keep till you get here."

"Ten minutes," Rhodes said, and hung up the mike.

It was getting late when Rhodes got back to the jail, though it was still well over an hour until dark. He parked the car and went inside.

Lawton was nowhere to be seen. Ruth Grady was talking to Hack about the radio. "It's amazing to me that you can operate something as complex as that," she said. "And to stay here all hours doing it! That must take real dedication."

Hack grinned. "I guess it does, at that," he said. " 'Course, I don't take too much money for it, either, being retired and all. I guess I'm just full of the public spirit."

Rhodes smiled. He knew that Ruth Grady could operate any radio ever made, or could learn to in about ten seconds, but she also knew the importance of a good working relationship within the department. And she would obviously do whatever she had to do to get it. Not that it hurt Hack to be praised. Rhodes himself probably didn't do it often enough. He reminded himself to try to improve.

"Well," Rhodes said, "what's the big news that didn't need to go out over the radio?"

"You'd better give him your news first, Hack," Ruth said.

"Aw, mine's not so important," Hack said. "I . . . uh . . . I'll wait till later."

"No, go ahead," Ruth told him. "A crime ought to be reported as soon as possible."

"Well, you couldn't exactly call it a crime," Hack

said. "I mean, it seemed like a crime at first, but it weren't one after all."

Rhodes noticed to his surprise that Hack seemed to be blushing. He was suddenly very curious. "Ruth's right, Hack. Let's have it."

"Well . . . uh . . . we got this call from Mrs. Wheelis over on Stem Street." Hack stopped. "It was really all just a mistake," he said at last.

"What?" Rhodes asked. "*What* was just a mistake?"

"The dead body," Hack said.

"Dead body? There was a dead body?" Rhodes found his voice rising a little. Then he looked at Ruth Grady, who was suppressing a smile.

"No, no," Hack said. "There wasn't no body. She just thought there was."

"I see," Rhodes said, though he didn't.

"It was her little boy that found it," Hack said.

"Found what?" Rhodes asked. "The body?"

"Wasn't no body. I just told you that. It was what he *thought* was a body."

Rhodes had never allowed himself to become exasperated with Hack, and he wasn't going to start now. "Fine," he said. "What was it?"

Hack looked at Ruth, who was looking away. Rhodes had the distinct impression that she was trying not to laugh.

"Buddy checked it out," Hack said. "You know that dirt road that joins Stem to Bud Street in about the 1500 block? Well, the Wheelis boy was walking down that road, kickin' a can or somethin', when he spotted it in the ditch."

Now they were getting somewhere, Rhodes thought. "Spotted what in the ditch?" he asked.

"What he thought was a body," Hack said. "His mother thought so, too. She went down there and looked before she called us."

Ruth apparently couldn't stand the suspense any longer. "It was a doll," she said.

"A doll?" Rhodes was even more confused.

Hack was blushing. "It was one of them, what you call 'em. . . ."

"An inflatable doll," Ruth said. "I think they call them 'sexual aids.' Apparently it was fairly anatomically accurate."

"Oh," Rhodes said.

"Trash," Hack said. "The whole world is just full of trash these days. Who'd throw a thing like that on the road where a kid might run across it? Can you tell me that? Trash, that's who."

Rhodes wasn't sure, now, whether Hack's ears were red from blushing or from anger. He tried not to laugh. "Did Buddy . . . ah . . . take care of the problem?"

"I think he stuck a hole in it," Hack said. "He didn't like it no better than I did. He'll be bringin' it in, I guess, for evidence."

"Never a dull moment," Rhodes said.

Hack snorted and turned back to his radio. Rhodes walked over to Ruth Grady. "Now what's the information you have?" he asked.

"It may not be too important," Ruth said, "but I found out something about motorcycles. It has to do with a woman named Wyneva Greer."

"Let's go over and sit at my desk," Rhodes said.

After they were seated, he asked, "What did you find out?" He was careful not to ask from whom the information came.

"Well, from what I hear, the Greer woman came to town seven or eight months ago. Not too long after that, she moved in with Bert Ramsey. The interesting part is, I think she used to be the old lady of a member of a motorcycle gang. The words Los Muertos were mentioned."

"That's interesting, all right," Rhodes said. He leaned back, and the chair squeaked. Hack looked up.

"I'll be right back," Ruth said. She stood up and walked to the door.

"What's she up to?" Hack asked, having turned around now.

"I don't know," Rhodes said, but by then Ruth was back, with a can of WD-40 in her right hand. "I carry a can of this stuff in the car," she said.

She knelt down and looked under Rhodes's chair. "Lean up," she said. Rhodes leaned up, and as he did Ruth gave the chair's spring a shot of the lubricant, which hissed out of the thin, red plastic tube stuck in the white plastic top. "Now lean back again."

Rhodes leaned back, and the chair squeaked only a little. He went forward, and the squeak was gone.

"That's good stuff," Hack said. "I was gettin' mighty tired of havin' to listen to that noise every time the sheriff sat down." Rhodes could tell that his respect for Ruth had risen another notch.

Ruth put the can down on Rhodes's desk. "Now," she said. "I think my information's accurate. I think Wyneva Greer is a hanger-on of the Los Muertos boys, and besides, before she took up with Ramsey, she was seen here and there with some real heavy-leather boys."

"Apparently, they've been around," Rhodes said. "I don't know why nobody told me about them."

"Maybe they kept a low profile," Ruth said. "My informant doesn't exactly hang around places where sheriff's deputies spend their time, and she certainly isn't the type to call up this office to tell us there's a gang member in town."

"I guess not," Rhodes said. "I wonder where Wyneva Greer knew Bert Ramsey from?"

He didn't expect an answer, and Ruth didn't have one. "I don't know," she said. "My informant wasn't close to her. She was just telling me something she'd seen and heard."

"I understand," Rhodes said. "And thanks, Ruth. You've given me something to think about."

"What about the various body parts found lying around the county?" Ruth asked. "Have you managed to get rid of them, yet?"

"Not yet," Rhodes said. "But I think Clyde Ballinger is going to take care of things. I talked to him and the doctor from Houston this morning, and I think they worked something out."

"I hope so. I hate to think of things like that lying around unburied. It's just gruesome, or something." She paused. "I wonder why Bert Ramsey didn't just burn them?"

"I've wondered the same thing," Rhodes said. "There was something funny going on with Bert, obviously. Why would he call attention to himself by reporting those boxes? Why not just keep quiet?"

"Unless what he was involved in wasn't so bad," Ruth said. "I mean, not as bad as severed body parts."

"It was bad," Rhodes said. "It got him killed."

"I see what you mean. It's worrisome, though."

"It certainly is. Obviously I need to have another talk with Wyneva Greer."

"You've met her?" Ruth sounded disappointed.

"I've met her," Rhodes said. "But I haven't talked to her. I guess I misled you. I talked to the man she's living with, but not to her. She didn't say a word. Thanks to what you've told me, though, I can see that she probably has a few things she could tell me."

"Maybe I could talk to her," Ruth said.

"No, I'll talk to her myself. I've already been out there once. I don't want her and Buster Cullens to think I've assigned every officer in the county to them." Rhodes knew that he was telling only half the truth. He also didn't want Ruth Grady getting involved in a murder case, not when he suspected that Buster Cullens was the killer. I'm almost as bad as Hack, Rhodes thought.

Heavy black clouds were massing in the northeastern sky when Rhodes left the jail just before nightfall. He thought that he detected a hint of a cool breeze. Maybe the dry spell was about to break.

He got in the county car. He had told Ivy that he would come by, and he felt a little chill up his spine. He'd necked with her just like a schoolboy, and he hadn't been a boy in a lot of years. He knew that to many people a little necking didn't mean a thing. Times had changed a great deal since he was a high-school kid. But he hadn't changed, try as he might. He was still an old-fashioned man, with old-fashioned ideas, at least about a lot of things. One thing was women. In his way of thinking, you didn't lead women on, not women like Ivy. You were honest with them, and you declared your intentions.

Unfortunately, he still wasn't quite sure what his intentions were. Did he want to get married again, or not? Was it worth the risk of doing again? There was a lot to gain, but there was a lot to lose, as he had already discovered once, the hard way.

If Kathy were there, she would have told him to marry, he was pretty sure. When she'd taken the teaching job, she had said that she knew she was leaving him in good hands. There was no mistaking her meaning. She clearly expected him to marry Ivy, and she just as clearly approved. Rhodes was pretty sure he approved, too. Last night, he'd been absolutely sure. Now, he was wavering again. *I didn't know I was so wishy-washy,* he thought.

Ivy came to the door wearing jeans and a checked shirt. She'd had a haircut, and her hair was very short. She'd done nothing about the gray that flecked the blackness, and Rhodes approved.

80

"Notice anything?" she asked.

"Besides the haircut?" Rhodes asked. "I like it, by the way."

"No, not the haircut," Ivy said, tilting her head.

Rhodes saw the gold ball on her left earlobe. "My lord," he said, "you've had your ears pierced."

Ivy took his hands and pulled him into the house. "That's right," she said. "I just thought, better late than never. They do it right there at the beauty parlor. It was an impulse, I guess. I think I've always wanted pierced ears, but I never had the nerve to get it done. What do you think?"

Rhodes was feeling like a kid again, and he wasn't exactly sure what to say. When he had been young, 'nice' girls weren't the ones with pierced ears. But that had been a long time ago. Surely he wasn't *that* old-fashioned, was he?

"I like it," he said. And he did. "I'll have to get you a pair of earrings with diamonds."

Ivy was pleased. "You're sure? You don't think I'm a hussy?"

Rhodes laughed aloud. Ivy looked so young, and made him feel so young, that he kept forgetting that she was nearly his own age. She must have had the same thought he had. "Of course not," he said. "How could anyone think that? It never entered my mind." A good thing no one can arrest the sheriff for lying, he thought. Anyway, it's just a white lie.

"Liar," Ivy laughed. She led him over to the couch, a not very comfortable model covered in thick gold cloth.

"Well, maybe the thought did cross my mind," Rhodes said. "You know, a man of my generation. . . ."

"Never mind," Ivy said. "Tell me all the hot gossip of the county."

Rhodes told her about the doll that the Wheelis boy had found in the ditch. "Buddy's not the most liberal-minded man in town, you know. Not too long ago he tried to charge a couple with adultery. I'd bet that by the time he turns in the evidence, it's flatter than a pancake and rolled into a little ball."

Ivy laughed at the story, but she wanted to know about the murder investigation. Rhodes told her about the four men at the Gottschalk place, and he told her that Bert Ramsey's funeral would be the next day.

"I'd like to go," she said.

Rhodes was surprised. "Why?"

"I don't know. I guess I feel sorry for Mrs. Ramsey. She seemed so sad when we talked to her."

"Can you get off work?"

"I think so. What time?"

"Ten o'clock."

"Can you pick me up, or shall I go by myself?"

"I'll pick you up," Rhodes said. "I'll be there on official business, but there's no reason I shouldn't let you go with me."

"Fine. I'll be ready."

Just at that moment, a bolt of lightning shot across the sky, lighting up the darkness outside. It was followed almost at once by a tremendously loud roll of thunder. The lights flickered and went out.

"Must have hit a transformer," Rhodes said lamely.

"Where was Moses when the lights went out?" Ivy asked.

"I remember that one from the eleventh grade," Rhodes said. "From *Huckleberry Finn*. He was in the dark. Just like us." The eleventh hour, he thought. Oh, lord. He put his arm up on the back of the couch. He could barely see Ivy, but she was there. Oh, lord, he thought again.

10

RHODES WAS SURE of two things the next morning. One was that he was not making much progress in finding out who had killed Bert Ramsey. The thought of attending the funeral brought that fact home, hard. So far, Rhodes had talked to Buster Cullens for a few minutes and learned nothing. He had also talked to four members of Los Muertos and learned even less.

Why would Los Muertos want to kill Ramsey, anyway? Rhodes had no idea, and he certainly had no hard evidence that they were involved in any way at all. Mrs. Ramsey had heard motorcycles. That was it.

And what about Buster Cullens? Again, he had Mrs. Ramsey's story that Buster was now living with Bert's old girl friend, along with Mrs. Ramsey's strong feeling that Buster was guilty. And that was all. There was nothing to link the two men in any other way.

What bothered Rhodes most was the money in Bert's house, along with all the evidence of a lot of spending. Bert hadn't earned all the money by doing odd jobs.

The other thing that Rhodes was sure of was that he was now an engaged man. Or maybe he wasn't. He couldn't remember exactly what he'd said, but it seemed to him that he'd made some pretty definite promises. He was engaged, all right. Of course, they hadn't set a date or anything like that. He wished he could remember his exact words.

It didn't really matter, however. Rhodes still felt like a

teenager, and he also felt inordinately pleased with himself. He'd have to call Kathy and let her know.

He had a bowl of Grape Nuts, got dressed in khakis, and rode down to the jail. There was not much going on. A nursing home patient was missing, but he had wandered off before, and no one was really worried yet. There had been a bit of vandalism at the high school, but nothing that couldn't be fixed. Rhodes caught up on his reports and then went to pick up Ivy.

Ivy was dressed in a dark gray suit, and Rhodes was once again impressed with her trim figure. She made no reference to the previous night, and neither did Rhodes. It didn't seem like the proper time.

The rainfall had settled the dust and greened up the grass, and the northerly breeze that had pushed in behind it had cooled the weather down to an almost bearable temperature. The cemetery would be muddy, but probably not too bad.

They arrived at Ballinger's. Rhodes parked in front, this time, and they went in. They signed the register and sat in the back of the small chapel. Rhodes didn't like funerals.

The organist played a series of the slowest, most maudlin tunes imaginable—"In the Garden," "Sunrise," "The Old Rugged Cross." Rhodes was going to make out a list of upbeat numbers for his own funeral and request that they be played at top speed. He was considering "The Uncloudy Day" and "When the Roll Is Called Up Yonder" when the rest of the small crowd began to trickle in.

Rhodes recognized some of them, people for whom Ramsey had worked, for the most part, except for old Tink Lindsey and his wife. Attending funerals was their only form of entertainment, and Clyde Ballinger had once told Rhodes that the Lindseys hadn't missed a funeral at his establishment in the last fifteen years.

The minister came in and stood beside the open casket. Then the family came in and was seated in an alcove just off to the left of the main section of the chapel. There were Mrs. Ramsey and two men. Rhodes didn't know the men, but he assumed they were uncles or cousins.

The minister had just begun to speak about "the dear departed" when Wyneva Greer came in. She was wearing a pair of tight jeans and a faded blue shirt. She walked down near the front and took a seat.

The minister began talking about how he had searched for a scripture appropriate to the life of a man like Bert Ramsey, someone who'd made his livelihood by helping others. "In the course of my search," he said, "I came across Chapter 4 of Ephesians, in which Paul says . . ."

It was at this point that Mrs. Ramsey looked up and saw Wyneva Greer. "Get that woman out of here," she said, in a stage whisper.

The preacher stopped abruptly in his talk. "Preach on, preacher," Mrs. Ramsey said. "Get that woman out of here," she hissed to one of the men beside her.

The preacher, unable to figure out just exactly what was happening, remained silent. "Preach on, preacher," Mrs. Ramsey said again.

The minister tried to pick up the thread of his talk. "Ah . . . now in Ephesians, Paul speaks of how people have different abilities, and of how some are put here for service . . ."

Neither of the men by Mrs. Ramsey had made a move, so she hauled her bulk up and squeezed herself out between the narrow pews, heading for Wyneva. The minister stopped again.

"Preach on," Mrs. Ramsey said over her shoulder.

The minister stood with his mouth open, but nothing came out.

Wyneva sat stolidly, watching Mrs. Ramsey approach.

Ivy's elbow touched Rhodes lightly in the ribs. Rhodes

had had a bad experience at the last funeral of a murder victim he'd attended, one which he wasn't eager to repeat. He got up, and he started for Wyneva Greer.

Mrs. Ramsey got there first and reached for Wyneva's shoulders with her huge hands. Before she could get a solid grip, Rhodes brushed her arms aside, took Wyneva's arm and pulled her into the aisle.

"I got a right to be here," Wyneva said.

"You ain't got no rights at all, you godless hussy," Mrs. Ramsey said. "Bert wouldn't be here if it wasn't for you. Get on out of here, right now!" She turned back to the minister. "And you get on with your preachin'," she said.

Rhodes noticed the Lindseys, who were sitting with rapt expressions on their faces. He would have bet that they were enjoying this funeral more than any one they'd attended in the past fifteen years. He increased his pull on Wyneva's arms, and she reluctantly gave ground. By the time Mrs. Ramsey got turned to face them again, Rhodes had backed Wyneva nearly all the way to the rear of the chapel.

Mrs. Ramsey appeared satisfied. Rather than working her way back to the family section, she sat in the nearest pew. "Get on with it, preacher," she said.

The preacher cleared his throat, and as Rhodes was pulling Wyneva through the back door the message was beginning again.

Clyde Ballinger, who had come around from his spot near the family, was waiting for Rhodes and Wyneva when they left the chapel. "I swear I never saw anything like that," Ballinger said. "That old woman was on a real tear."

Wyneva jerked her arm free of Rhodes's grip. "Crazy old bat," she said. "I got as much right as the next person to sit in there."

"You have a right," Rhodes said, "but I have a feeling

that if you go back in there, there won't be much of a service."

"You can walk around with me and listen by the family section," Ballinger said.

Wyneva shook her head. "That's all right. I guess it was a mistake for me to come here. I'm going outside for some air." She started for the big double door in the front of the building. Rhodes followed along.

"Mrs. Ramsey really has it in for you," Rhodes said when they were outside on the long cement porch. "Do you have any idea why?"

"Sure I do," Wyneva said. "She thought I corrupted her precious boy. Well, she's sure wrong about that." She stopped. "Buster said I wasn't to talk to you, though."

"Buster doesn't have anything to do with this, does he?" Rhodes asked.

"I can't say." Wyneva stepped off the porch and started down the walk. When Rhodes followed, she began to run. She was faster than he would have thought, and he really didn't want to leave Ivy alone. He could talk to Wyneva later, so he let her go.

He went back inside the funeral home, but he didn't enter the chapel. He'd never liked the end of the service, where everyone had to walk down the aisle and take a last long look at the dead. He'd seen enough of death in its natural state, but he thought that the efforts of morticians did little to improve things. If anything, the distortion of life that they produced repelled Rhodes as much or more than the real thing. Not that he'd ever tell Clyde Ballinger that.

While he waited, he decided to go to the graveside service, which was to be held at the little cemetery by the Eller's Prairie Baptist Church. After the service, he could go have another talk with Wyneva and with Buster Cullens.

Rhodes walked out to his car and got Hack on the radio. "Call Buddy off the funeral traffic detail," he said. "I'll work it myself."

"Roger," Hack said.

"What?"

"Roger," Hack repeated.

"Oh," Rhodes said. "Over and out." Hack must have been talking to Ruth Grady again. He wondered if she'd brought in another cake.

The first mourners, if that was the proper term, began to leave the funeral home, and Rhodes went back up on the porch to wait for Ivy. "Did the rest go all right?" he asked when she came out the door.

"As right as those things go," she said. "Who was that poor woman?"

"I thought Mrs. Ramsey was the one you felt sorry for," Rhodes said.

"Not anymore. Who was that?"

"That was Wyneva Greer, former live-in girl friend of the late Bert Ramsey."

"Oh," Ivy said.

"I'm going on to the graveside," Rhodes said. "Do you want me to run you by home first?"

"I have the whole day off," Ivy said. "I don't mind spending a little more time with you. It's never dull."

"It usually is," Rhodes said. "Just wait till you're around me all the time."

Ivy looked at him closely. "I'm actually looking forward to that a lot," she said.

Rhodes blushed. "Let's get in the car," he said.

While the hearse was being loaded from the rear of the chapel, Rhodes and Ivy drove to the only intersection of Clearview that would need traffic control. Rhodes stopped the car and got out, and as the short funeral procession approached he held up a hand to stop the cars on the side street. There were only three, two on one side of the intersection and one on the other, and they would probably have stopped without Rhodes's being there.

There were only seven cars in the procession, counting the hearse. When they had passed, all with their lights on, Rhodes got back in with Ivy, turned on his own lights, and followed along.

When they were only about a mile out of Clearview, Rhodes heard the motorcycles. There were four, and they came roaring up behind the procession at more than fifty miles an hour. Rhodes could hear the thunder of their pipes even though he had the windows up and the air conditioner on.

There were four bikes, all in a single line. As they zipped by the car, Rhodes had no time to look closely at the riders, but he figured he knew who they were.

The bikes sped by all the cars in the procession, and luckily there was no one coming in the other direction. When each rider drew even with the long, black hearse, he did a wheelie, gliding past the hearse with the front wheel of the bike in the air. As the front wheel touched the road again, each rider gunned his engine and swung back into the right lane of the road. Rhodes couldn't see them after that, but the diminishing sound of their exhausts told him that they were rapidly pulling ahead.

"Aren't you going to arrest those hooligans?" Ivy asked.

"Nope. They saw me just as clearly as we saw them," Rhodes said. "And they know I'm not going to disrupt this funeral procession to go chasing after them. It's just their formal salute to a departed member, I guess. Nothing to make a fuss about."

"It seemed awfully dangerous to me," Ivy said.

"Dangerous for them, yes. Not for anybody else, as long as the lane was clear." Rhodes didn't mention that he suspected the four riders of crimes a lot more serious than reckless driving. "Their day will come. Maybe I can get them for jaywalking."

"Maybe," Ivy said, but Rhodes could tell she didn't like it.

The burial site looked like a picture from a magazine. The rain had freshened the grass, and the tombstones looked newly cleaned, sparkling white in the late morning sun. The little church was white too, and so close by that with its white steeple it added a note of gravity to the scene. The ground was still wet from the rain, but not muddy enough to be a bother to the men. The women in heels had a problem, however.

Everything was arranged by the time Rhodes and Ivy got to the graveside. The minister read from Ecclesiastes about the sun also arising and began his brief remarks.

Rhodes heard the motorcycles. He looked over his shoulder and saw them coming down the muddy country road.

The preacher, heeding Mrs. Ramsey's advice from the chapel, preached on as best he could over the noise.

The motorcycles stopped beside the cars, their engines idling.

"Moreover," the minister was saying, "though Bert Ramsey is not with us, yet his spirit lives. For God is the God of the living; He is not the God of the dead."

Rapper's voice cut through the air. "That's what you think, preacher. Once you're one of Los Muertos, you're always one of Los Muertos. And Ramsey was sure one of us!"

Everyone had turned to watch Rapper. The four bikers revved their engines and skidded away, slinging mud from the spinning rear tires.

The minister stared after them with his mouth open.

Rhodes looked at Mrs. Ramsey. Her mouth was a

tight, white line in her puffy face. He looked at the Lindseys. They could hardly contain themselves. Whatever they'd seen in the last fifteen years, nothing would ever come up to this day.

The preacher finally recovered himself and finished as quickly as he decently could. The casket was being lowered into the open grave as Ivy and Rhodes made their way back to the car.

"I really wish you could do something about those men," Ivy said when they were in the car.

"I'm not sure what I can do," Rhodes said.

Ivy didn't say anything.

"Since we're so close, I might ride down and say a few words to Buster Cullens," Rhodes said. "He might know those guys. Want to go along?"

"Do I have a choice?" Ivy was not being sarcastic. She was obviously curious.

"Sure. I can take you back to town."

"Too much bother. I'll just stay in the car and you can do all your interrogating."

"Wyneva may be there. I thought she'd come back here after she left the chapel, but I guess she'd had enough."

"I wouldn't blame her," Ivy said.

"I wonder how she got there?" Rhodes said. "I didn't see hide nor hair of Buster Cullens."

"Maybe she walked."

"Not from here; this road's a mess." Rhodes wasn't exaggerating. The road had been dusty before, but the rain had rutted it with mud, which, though not deep enough to cause a real hazard, still made driving difficult. Rhodes held the car firmly in the ruts to avoid sliding sideways into the ditch.

Rhodes saw the motorcycles in Buster Cullens's yard before he turned in at the open gap. "Looks like Buster and Wyneva have company," he said. He stopped the car and got out. The soil of the yard was of a different consistency from that of the road, blacker and stickier. It slopped up over Rhodes's shoes.

"You better wait," Rhodes told Ivy.

"That's what I planned to do, remember?"

"Yeah." Rhodes started toward the dilapidated house, slopping through the mud. He stopped outside the front door beside the motorcycles. "Cullens!" he yelled. "You in there?"

There was no answer. The day suddenly seemed to get warmer and more oppressive as the silence lengthened. "Cullens!" Rhodes called again. "Rapper! Who's in there?"

There was still no reply, and Rhodes took another step closer to the door, his feet lifting from the mud with a sucking sound.

"Cullens? If you're in there, sing out. Otherwise, I'm coming in. I don't like standing in the mud." Rhodes wasn't particularly keen on the idea of going inside the house, not knowing just where Rapper was located or what, if anything, was happening to Buster Cullens.

Then Rhodes heard a high-pitched groan and the sound of something falling to the floor. He didn't wait any longer. He stepped up on the porch and opened the screen door. When he stepped into the house, his short-barreled .38 was in his hand. The dog! he thought. What about the dog? Then something hit him on the back, hard, and he was on the floor. The gun was no longer in his hand, and something hit him again.

"Kill him!" someone yelled. "Kill the sonofabitch!"

It was Rapper.

11

RHODES HAD NO intention of letting anyone kill him, not with Ivy sitting in the car, not if he could help it. He rolled over on his back, which he hoped wasn't broken, just in time to see Jayse swinging an axe handle at him. He put up his hands to take the blow and was able to get a grip on the handle. Pulling with the force of the blow, he threw Jayse off balance.

Jayse stumbled and Rhodes kicked upward at his stomach. It wasn't much of a kick, but Jayse lost his hold on the handle. Rhodes didn't. He got himself into a sitting position and swung the handle at Jayse's shins as if he were Reggie Jackson trying for one more long ball. He got the left one.

The sound was horrible, but not as horrible as the scream Jayse let out before he collapsed on the floor. He screamed and cried as Rhodes struggled to his feet and through the door into the back room.

Rapper, Nellie, and the fourth man were there. Buster Cullens was on the floor, a gag around his head. Rhodes couldn't tell if he was alive or dead. He wasn't moving.

When Rhodes came through the door with the axe handle, the scene appeared frozen. Obviously, the three men were expecting Jayse. They didn't know who was yelling in the next room, but they'd thought it was Rhodes. When they realized it wasn't, they went into motion.

Nellie and the other man charged Rhodes, who swung the handle. It hit the man whose name Rhodes hadn't learned in the head with a sound like hitting a watermelon with a drumstick. The man dropped like a sack of horse and mule feed, but Nellie caught Rhodes on his follow-through and drove him back into the room where Jayse lay clutching his shin and whimpering.

Rhodes smashed into the wall hard enough to bring a shower of dust and dirt from the ceiling overhead. Pain shot through his already sore back, and he was momentarily stunned, unable to move or even lift the axe handle.

Nellie was looking around the bare room for something to hit him with when his eyes fell on Rhodes's pistol. He started for it just as Rapper came into the room. "Let me have it," Rapper said, stooping to pick it up. His face was red and distorted. He looked dangerously out of control.

Rhodes got his breath and stepped up to hit Nellie, who was between him and Rapper. But Rhodes was still stunned, and Nellie had other ideas. He stepped under Rhodes's feeble swing and hit Rhodes in the stomach. Hard.

Rhodes staggered backward, but this time he missed the wall. Instead, he hit the screen door, which, because it was hinged to swing out, offered no resistance at all.

Rhodes tried to gain his balance, but it was as if his feet were no longer under the direction of his brain. He staggered on to the small porch and over the edge, falling flat on his back in the mud.

Nellie and Rapper were right behind him. Rhodes managed to get his feet under him somehow, but he slipped back in the mud almost at once, which was just as well, since the three shots that Rapper fired zipped over him. Rhodes heard three loud clanking and clanging noises, and the bullets plowed into the grille and radiator and fan and probably the engine block of the county car.

"Goddamngoddamngoddamn!" Rapper yelled, the words running together in his rage. He sounded as if he might be strangling.

Rhodes heard two more shots. The first smacked solidly into the mud beside him. The second shattered glass. Ivy!

There were no more bullets. Rhodes stood up, and Nellie dived on him. As they were going down, Rhodes heard a car door slam. Ivy was all right, he thought. Then he heard her yelling. The door slammed again. Then he and Nellie were wrestling in the mud, rolling around, trying to get a hold or a solid lick. Rhodes had lost the axe handle.

Rhodes and Nellie rolled over and over. They were slick as pond scum, covered with mud. Finally, Rhodes got on top and managed a hard pop at Nellie's jaw. Then Rapper threw a body block into him and he sailed off.

Rapper jerked Nellie out of the mud and they lurched toward the motorcycles. Rhodes got up and looked toward the car. Ivy opened the door and got out.

The bikes started and Rapper and Nellie roared away, slewing through the mud. They headed across the field rather than toward the road.

"The car's had it," Rhodes said. "The radio. . . ."

"That man tried to get in and rip out the mike," Ivy said. "But I slammed the door. Got it locked, too. Then he broke the aerial off."

"Damn," Rhodes said. "There's no way to get them now." He looked at the other two bikes. "First time I ever wanted to be able to ride one of those things. Never learned how."

"I did," Ivy said. "Come on."

"What?"

"I can ride one. My brother had one. Come on."

Rhodes watched in amazement as Ivy walked over to

the nearest motorcycle, hiked her skirt up to her hips, and straddled it. "Come on!" she said again. "They'll get completely away!"

He walked over, still not sure he wasn't dreaming. On the way he stooped to pick up his pistol, which Rapper had dropped. The thought occurred to him that Ivy's legs were even better than he would have guessed. He straddled the bike behind her, and even his thoughts were drowned out by its roar as she started it.

As they sped out of the yard in pursuit of Rapper and Nellie, Rhodes began to think he was living in a bad remake of *Born Losers*. "Are you sure . . . ?" he yelled in Ivy's ear.

"Put your arms around me," she yelled back. "I'm sure."

Rhodes did as he was told.

The fields across which they were riding had not been plowed in years, but it was still rough and rutted. At times, the motorcycle seemed to leave the ground by several feet, and every time it landed, Rhodes felt the shock from the base of his spine, right up through his sore back, and on up through the top of his head. He hung on tight.

After only a minute, he could tell that Ivy was actually gaining on Rapper and Nellie. He wasn't surprised. They were only criminals. They weren't crazy, which you had to be to drive like Ivy was.

Then the two men came to a barbed wire fence. They made a sharp right turn. Ivy didn't slow down.

Rhodes closed his eyes. He couldn't even imagine what it would be like to hit the fence.

"Lean with me!" Ivy yelled. Rhodes felt her weight shift and shifted his own to match it. They made a sharp right turn, throwing up a raft of mud against the fence post which seemed to Rhodes to be within inches of the wheel. As they straightened out and headed down the fence row, Rhodes realized that he had been thinking of the wrong movie. This wasn't *Born Losers*. He was in fact hanging on to Steve McQueen during his race for life in *The Great Escape*. He hoped that Ivy didn't plan to try jumping the fence.

Rapper and Nellie, however, were planning exactly that. They hooked another right, then another, heading back the way they'd come, except that they were about a hundred yards from the fence. By the time that Ivy had made another turn, they were gunning straight for the fence, or more accurately for a small rise of dirt just in front of it, which they must have spotted earlier.

Rapper's bike was in the lead. He hit the rise, elevating his front wheel, and took off as if on a ramp. He sailed over the fence, Nellie right behind him. Their bikes hit, slewed wildly through the mud, righted, and took off.

Ivy slowed to a stop. "I can't make it with two of us," she said.

Rhodes was quietly thankful. He might have fired after them if he'd had time to load his gun before they were out of sight, but he didn't. Instead, he said, "Let's go on back to the house and see what we can find out."

The trip back was not quite so hectic, and Rhodes had time to marvel at Ivy's hidden talents. She was also a lot tougher than he'd thought. He should have known better than to judge her.

When they got back to the house, Jayse was still lying on the floor. He was no longer moaning or whimpering, however. He had passed out. Rhodes had broken his leg.

The man in the back room, the one whose name Rhodes hadn't learned, had returned to consciousness, but only barely.

Buster Cullens lay where he had fallen. He was dead.

Ivy helped Rhodes search the house. The other two rooms contained nearly nothing. There was a bed, surprisingly neatly made up. There was a chest of drawers containing a few changes of clothing for Cullens and Wyneva. That was it. No place to cook. Nothing else. There was no form of identification for Cullens, not even in his pants pockets. There was a little money, about fifteen dollars. That was all.

"They must have eaten out a lot," Rhodes said.

Ivy looked at him and laughed.

"What's so funny?" he asked.

"You know when that man was trying to get in the car? You were rolling around in all that mud, and all I could think of was the fight scene in *North to Alaska*. You should see yourself now."

"You like *North to Alaska?*"

"Even Fabian."

Rhodes felt mud crack on his face as he grinned. "I knew you were a woman of taste," he said. "Now there's a little favor I have to ask."

"First the compliment, then the favors," Ivy said.

"Well, for that matter you aren't so clean yourself," Rhodes said.

"Never mind. What's the favor."

"Ride that thing down to Mrs. Ramsey's and call the J.P., the ambulance, and Hack. I'll stay here and watch things."

"I could watch."

"Don't start," Rhodes said. "Nobody likes a smart aleck."

"All right, I'll make your calls. Anything else?"

"Yeah. Bring back the bike. It's evidence."

They went outside. Standing off to one side, his tail between his legs, was the dog. He eyed them with suspicion.

Rhodes knelt on the porch and whistled. The dog came forward a step or two, then stopped. "C'mon, boy," Rhodes said.

After continued coaxing, he managed to get the dog to

come to him. He ran his hand over its head. There was a large lump. "That Jayse sure liked that axe handle," Rhodes said. He rubbed the dog.

"Is he one of the men you hurt?" Ivy asked.

"Yeah, the one in the front room."

"Good," Ivy said. She walked over to the motorcycle. "I'll be right back."

"Take your time," Rhodes said. "I won't be going anywhere."

Back in the house, Rhodes inspected Cullens's body. Bruises had formed around his kidneys and abdomen where he'd been repeatedly struck. Rhodes wondered if Rapper had been taking revenge because of Wyneva. Maybe she was like Bert Ramsey. Once you were one of the dead, you were always one of the dead. Rapper seemed just the kind of man to kill out of jealousy or revenge.

This was clearly different from Bert Ramsey's death, though. Cullens had been tortured. There was generally only one reason for torture, and that was to gain information. What information did Cullens have that Rapper wanted? And had Rapper gotten it?

Rhodes tied up the nameless man with a belt he found in the chest of drawers. Jayse was still out. He hoped they'd be able to answer his questions. He'd give a lot, sometimes, to be like the stereotypical Texas sheriff in movies and cheap novels, with a sadistic deputy and a cattle prod to use on recalcitrant prisoners. Unfortunately, he couldn't work like that.

He went back out on the porch. The dog was still there, and he rubbed its head. He figured the dog could tell him a lot if it could only discuss things with him. It could probably have told him, for instance, where Wyneva was. Obviously, she hadn't come back here after the funeral fiasco at Ballinger's chapel, which was probably for the best. Rapper might have finished her off, too. He might be looking for her even now.

Rhodes's back ached. He knew he'd have a huge bruise on it by the next day. Besides, he was covered with mud. If Cullens had had indoor plumbing, Rhodes would have washed off, but there was only an old well in the backyard.

Thinking of the well put another, much less pleasant, thought in Rhodes's mind. He went around to the back, the dog at his heels. When he got to the well, he lifted the cover off and looked down. It was just a well, and he could see light reflect off the water below. For a minute, he'd been afraid that Rapper had thrown Wyneva down there.

Since he was already there, Rhodes let down the galvanized bucket and drew it back up. The water was clear and cold, and he washed off his hands and face as best he could.

Then he heard the motorcycle returning and went back around to the front. He still found it a little hard to believe that Ivy could ride the bike so well.

She came to a stop near the porch, got off, and reported. "Hack's sending Ruth Grady, and the ambulance and J.P. are on the way."

"Good," Rhodes said. "I'd like to get this all settled out."

"I'll bet," Ivy said. "Easier said than done."

"Maybe," Rhodes said. A pain shot across his back and he winced. "I seem to get a lot of roughing up without getting very good results."

"You've got two prisoners," Ivy reminded him.

"And another corpse," Rhodes said.

"Not to mention a dog," Ivy said, looking at the animal, which had followed Rhodes around to the front.

It sat a few yards away, its tongue hanging out. It was looking at Rhodes expectantly.

"Oh, no," Rhodes said. "Wait a minute."

"Somebody has to take care of it," Ivy said. "Surely you weren't planning just to leave it here to starve to death."

"Ah, well, I hadn't really thought about it, to tell the truth," Rhodes said.

"Well I had," Ivy said. "I think you should take it."

"I'll think about it," Rhodes said. "How was Mrs. Ramsey doing?"

Ivy's face clouded. "I'm not sure. I told her a little of what was going on here, and she started in about 'that Greer woman being to blame' and about how Bert had been a fine man until he met her. She was still upset about her being at the funeral, I could tell. She looked stony hard to me. I wouldn't want her coming at me like she went at Wyneva Greer this morning."

"I know what you mean," Rhodes said. "Let's check on our prisoners."

Neither man was in any condition to talk, but Rhodes figured they would both be in pretty good shape by the next day. He just hoped that he would. Now that he'd had time to stiffen up, it hurt him even to take a step. "What time is it, anyway?" he asked.

Ivy looked at her watch. "Nearly two o'clock."

"Seems like I never eat lunch anymore," Rhodes said.

"Now that you mention it. . . ."

"I guess in all the goings on, I kind of forgot," Rhodes said. "To tell the truth, I never thought about eating until right now."

"Me either," Ivy said.

The dog barked. "Him either," Rhodes said. He was almost resigned to having to adopt the dog. Then he remembered how the dog had come out from under the porch the first day he'd driven up. "Don't you need a good watchdog?"

"Watchdog?" Ivy was incredulous. "He didn't do Buster Cullens much good, did he?"

"I guess he didn't at that," Rhodes said. He shook his head and looked at the dog.

Then he looked down the road and saw the ambulance coming.

12

RHODES DID NOT like to ride in the car with dogs. He insisted that if it would be safe to leave the motorcycles in the country overnight, it would also be safe to leave the dog. "He's used to it here," he said.

It didn't do any good. Neither Ruth nor Ivy would listen to him, and so the dog was riding back to town with them in the county car. The fact that Rhodes had to share the back seat with him didn't help. "After all," Ruth told him, "you're at least as dirty as the dog."

Rhodes didn't point out that Ivy wasn't much cleaner. Probably, Ruth would have put the dog in front if he had. Ruth listened to the radio as she drove, a country station. Rhodes had once liked country music, but now it all sounded to him as if the singers were trying to get a job in a Vegas lounge. Occasionally there would be a song he'd like, but not often. It was the same with rock music. Rhodes had grown up with rock, and he had listened for hours to songs like those he'd played for Ivy a few nights before. But somewhere rock music had taken a turn that he had missed. The road forked, and he had taken the wrong fork. He seldom turned on the radio anymore.

So, what with having to sit in the back seat, the prisoner's seat, Rhodes thought ironically, and having to share the seat with the dog, and having to listen to Kenny Rogers croon through a forest of syrupy violins and cooing backup singers, Rhodes wasn't in a particularly good mood. Besides, he was dirty, and his back was sore. On top of everything, Rapper and Nellie had gotten away.

It didn't improve things when Ruth brought up Clyde Ballinger's latest telephone call. "Hack said you wouldn't like it," she said, explaining that Ballinger wanted to talk to Rhodes. Apparently, there was a hitch in the burial plans.

"Just drive by there right now," Rhodes told her.

"Now?" Ruth looked at him in the mirror.

Ivy turned in her seat and looked back through the grille that separated them. "Are you sure? I think if you had a bath and something to eat. . . ."

"I don't want a bath, and I don't want anything to eat," Rhodes said. "I want to get this mess settled."

"All right," Ruth said. "You're the sheriff."

For a minute or two, no one spoke. The dog lay quietly in the seat, his tongue hanging out.

"So," Ruth said finally, "what are you going to name the dog?"

"Don't start," Rhodes said. "Just don't start."

"It's a sensible question," Ivy said. "Are you sulking because I can ride a motorcycle better than you?"

"Of course not," Rhodes said. But then he wondered if maybe she had a point. "I think I may name the dog Carella."

"What?"

"Carella?"

"What kind of name is that?"

"Italian, I think."

"That's not what I meant, and you know it," Ivy said. "I meant, what kind of name is that for a dog to have?"

"I think it's kind of nice," Ruth said. "It has a nice sound."

"I like it," Rhodes said. He could hardly wait to tell Ballinger.

Ballinger liked the name, all right, but it didn't change his mind. "I can't bury them," he said. They were in his office, and he looked at Rhodes as if he wished Rhodes would disappear, or at least go home and change clothes. Ruth and Ivy were looking at the books that lined the shelves and not really listening. Every now and then they would pull one down and read the cover blurbs.

"You took Dr. Rawlings's money," Rhodes said. "You've got to bury them."

"I can send the money back," Ballinger said. "I've talked to my lawyer, and he says burying them would be a mistake. What if someone decided to sue?"

Rhodes sighed. It was the modern way. Everybody was suing everybody else. He supposed that even a mortician could be sued. "No one's going to sue," he said.

"How do you know?" Ballinger asked. He didn't ask in a smart way. He really wanted to know.

"Because all those limbs are from people who believe that they've already been disposed of." Rhodes didn't know if he was telling the truth, but it sounded plausible. "They're from amputees who paid someone to remove them. They were supposed to be burned. No one will ever know that you buried them."

"You're sure?"

"Rawlings hauled them off up here and dumped them in a pasture. You think a doctor would take a chance like that if there was even a remote possibility he could be sued?"

"You've got a point there," Ballinger said. "That lawyer of mine probably isn't as smart as he thinks. I'll do it."

"I hope so," Rhodes said. "I'm getting tired of thinking about those boxes. So give me an exact time. I want to be there."

Ballinger thought for a second. "Tomorrow evening, seven o'clock. The north end of the cemetery. No use calling any more attention to this than we have to." The north end of the cemetery was well back from the road and overlooked miles of open pasture.

"I'll be there," Rhodes said.

They left Ballinger and went back to the car, where the dog was waiting quietly. Ruth and Ivy were talking about the books.

"Can you believe there's really a book called *Guerrilla Girls?*" Ivy asked.

"How about *Backwoods Hussy?*" Ruth said.

"Don't laugh," Rhodes told them. "Some of those old books are pretty good."

Both women looked at him, but neither said a word. Rhodes sat in the back seat and rubbed the dog's head.

After he had bathed and eaten a sandwich, Rhodes felt better. Several ideas about what was going on were beginning to form, and while he didn't think he had all the answers, he did think he was getting a handle on things.

He went outside and looked at the dog, which seemed content to lie by the back steps. Of course, he'd eaten practically a whole package of Rhodes's bologna, so he certainly should have been content, at least for the time being. Rhodes knew he'd have to buy some real dog food pretty soon.

He had owned only one dog before, when Kathy was small. The dog's name was Speedo, for no good reason that Rhodes could remember. Like most dogs, Speedo had soon become like another member of the family and had lived with them happily for nearly ten years. Then one day he had run into the street, something he never did, and been hit by a passing car. Claire and Kathy had cried and cried—Kathy continued to sniffle for days— and Rhodes had taken Speedo into the backyard and buried him. Rhodes had cried a little, too. The rock that marked Speedo's grave still got in the way on those rare occasions when he mowed the backyard, but he'd never even given a thought to moving it. They had never gotten another dog.

"What the heck," Rhodes said to the dog. "You don't look Italian. I think I'll just call you Speedo. Nobody but you and I will know that your real name is Mr. Earl."

The dog, his tongue still hanging out slightly, looked at Rhodes. His tail thumped twice.

"That's settled, then," Rhodes said. He went back inside, ate another sandwich, using the last piece of his bologna, and went down to the jail.

"Hey, Sheriff," Hack said when Rhodes walked in. "What you drivin'?"

Rhodes didn't really want to think about the shot-up car he'd left at Buster Cullens's house. "I'm in my pickup," he said.

"Hear you got yourself a dog," Lawton said, "one with an Eye-talian name."

"His name's Speedo," Rhodes said. "I changed it."

"Oh," Lawton said. Whatever joke he'd planned about the dog's name was ruined.

Hack took up the slack. "Guess you heard about the demonstration."

Rhodes hadn't heard, of course.

"Big demonstration down by the phone company," Lawton said, wanting to get in on things. Hack looked at him and Lawton shut up.

"Lady called," Hack said. "She thought it might be commonists, wantin' to blow up the phone company."

"I didn't know there were enough Communists in Blacklin County to hold a demonstration," Rhodes said.

"You may be right," Hack said, "but I figured you'd want me to send somebody out to investigate."

"Absolutely right," Rhodes said. "We wouldn't want a Communist takeover right here in the middle of Texas."

"That's exactly what I thought," Hack said. "So I sent Buddy."

"That reminds me," Rhodes said. "What about that doll?"

"The evidence is safe," Lawton said. "Flatter than a flitter."

"About this here demonstration," Hack said.

"What about it?"

"You know where the Presbyterian church is?" Hack asked.

"That's the one where the Reverend Funk preaches," Lawton put in. Hack glared at him.

"Sure I know," Rhodes said. "What's that got to do—Wait a minute. There wouldn't have been a wedding there today, would there?"

Hack was a little disappointed that Rhodes had caught on. "Yeah, there was," he said. "Right catty-corner from the phone company. Looks like I sent Buddy down there to bust up a weddin' reception. They was all out on the walk, wavin' little bags of rice around and laughin' and goin' on. It prob'ly looked like a demonstration to somebody."

"I can see that," Rhodes said, not really sure that he could. "Did the caller give a name?"

"Nope. One o' those 'nonymous calls. Good thing, too. Whoever it was'll feel bad enough when she finds out, anyway."

"I doubt it," Rhodes said. "Whoever it was will just think it was a bunch of demonstrators disguised as a wedding party."

"You may be right, at that," Hack said.

"Well, it doesn't really matter," Rhodes said. "As long as it's taken care of. Now, have you sent a wrecker out for the county car?"

"Sure have. Commissioners are gonna love that. First

the air conditioner, and then the car. Bet our insurance goes up."

Rhodes changed the subject. "I'm going out to Gottschalk's place. You ever call him?"

"Yep. That Nellie is his nephew, all right. Hasn't seen him in years, though. Remembers him as a pretty good kid when he was little."

"Well, he's not little any more," Rhodes said.

"What you goin' out there for?" Lawton asked. "They surely won't be stayin' around after what happened this mornin'."

"I know that," Rhodes said. "They might have left something behind, though." He was pretty sure they hadn't. Rapper may have been psychotic, but he was smart. There wasn't anything else he could do today, however. He knew that the doctors at the hospital wouldn't let him do any serious questioning of Jayse and the other man until the next morning, after all the tests had been run and the injuries determined.

"Better take you some backup, just in case," Hack said.

"No need for that," Rhodes said. "They'll be long gone from there by now. I wouldn't be surprised if they were halfway to El Paso."

"All the same," Hack said.

"Don't worry," Rhodes told him. "There won't be any problem." He hoped he was right.

He was wrong, but he didn't know it at first. The sun was setting when he arrived at Gottschalk's and drove over the cattle guard, but there was still enough daylight left for Rhodes to see that the tent was gone, and that no motorcycles were parked anywhere around. He drove his pickup down to where the tent had been and parked it.

The ground was a good deal scuffed up where the tent

had been, but there hadn't been much rain here and things weren't in a really disturbed state. Rapper had probably been in a hurry, but not such a hurry as to leave things behind. Only in such a hurry as to move things quickly.

Rhodes scoured the ground and found nothing. He tried to trace the tracks of the bikes, but the ground was too torn up for that. As it began to get darker, he stopped looking and went to stand under the oak tree and look out at the water.

There was something about a tank at dusk that Rhodes really liked. Maybe it was the stillness of the water, or the quiet. Or maybe it was the way he could see a fish strike at a water bug every now and then, causing the water to pop and swirl for just a second or two. He thought briefly about getting his fishing rod out from behind the truck seat and making a few casts, but he told himself that would be too unprofessional. Still, it was a strong temptation.

He rested his sore back against the rough bark of the tree and soaked up the tranquillity for a while. Then, just as the first dark was settling in, he thought that he heard something.

It could have been just a trick of the quiet, but he didn't think so. He strained his ears and listened. After what seemed like quite a while, he heard something again. Voices.

Out in the country, in the late, late afternoon, when things are so still you'd think movement almost didn't exist, voices carry a long way. Even voices pitched low.

Rhodes wondered who could be in the pasture, but he figured he knew. Who else could it be? He should have looked for those tracks more carefully, he thought. He should have made a few circles, widening each one, around the campsite. Then he might have found out sooner. As it was, he'd almost missed it.

Rapper was smart, all right. Rather than risk finding another place to stay, he'd simply moved deeper into Gottschalk's property. He'd thought that anyone looking for him would accept the obvious fact that he was gone and then go look somewhere else. And he'd almost been right.

Rhodes eased up on top of the tank dam. It was mostly clay, softened a little by the rain, with a few bushes and weeds on top, just enough to offer a little cover if he kept low.

There wasn't much to see. Certainly there wasn't a tent, and there were no motorcycles. There was, however, a little copse of trees about four hundred yards away. In the gathering darkness, it was impossible to tell if there was a tent in there, but Rhodes would have bet there was.

Rhodes had absolutely no desire to slither on his stomach for four hundred yards. Instead, he went into a crouching run, from one bunch of milkweeds to the next, feeling he looked a little like Wile E. Coyote running along after a boulder had fallen on him.

He got to the edge of the woods, and he could hear the voices clearly by then, though they were slightly muffled and he still couldn't make out what was being said. He slipped his pistol out of its holster, stood up, and stepped behind the nearest tree. When he looked around it, he could see the dark outlines of the tent.

The rain had softened things up, and Rhodes thought he could make it to the tent without rustling the leaves. He just hoped that he didn't hang his pants leg on a thorny vine or step on a dead branch. He eased around the tree and crept forward, his pistol pointed at the tent.

He reached the tent easily. When he was near enough, he said, "All right, Rapper. You and Nellie come on out."

There was a brief shuffling around in the tent, and

Rhodes began to wonder if they were armed. In a second, however, Rapper and Nellie came out the front of the tent. They were crawling, since the tent was a small one. It was dark now, especially in the trees, but Rhodes could see no sign of a weapon in their hands.

"Well, you found us, Rhodes," Rapper said as he stood up. "I have to give you credit. You're smarter than I thought you were."

"Not smarter," Rhodes said. "Just luckier. Now if you two would just step apart a little. . . ." He motioned with the pistol, and the two men moved slightly apart. "A little farther . . . fine."

He moved over to Rapper to put the cuffs on him, all the time watching Nellie out of the corner of his eye. He had no idea that anyone could be behind him, but when he heard the slight rustle of the leaves he tried to turn. He was too late. The end of the tree limb hit him squarely on the side of the head.

13

RHODES WAS NOT out for long, but when he came to he was in no position to do much. He was lying face down on the ground, his face pressed into the tangy-smelling leaf mold. He couldn't move his arms, which were locked behind his back, held in place, he was sure, with his own handcuffs. It was embarrassing. His sore back was hurting more than ever, and the side of his head felt as if it had been caved in.

"I say we kill him right here." That was Nellie's voice. "Just shoot him in the back of the head with his own pistol and toss him in the tank. They'll find him if it ever dries up, if the turtles don't eat him first." Rhodes was beginning to develop a real dislike for Nellie.

"Don't be an idiot," Rapper said. "Someone knows he came here, and why he came here. If we kill a lawman, even one as sorry as this one, they'll hunt us forever. We'd never get a minute's rest."

Nellie laughed. "What we've done already ain't enough? Who's the idiot now? Look at him, trussed up like a pig."

"I hate to admit it, Nellie, but you may have a point," Rapper said in the voice of a man who really did hate to admit that someone else might have a better thought than his own. "Well, let's let him look at us when we do it. May as well get a little fun out of it."

Rhodes tensed himself. He didn't think he had a chance, because he didn't think he could move, but he wasn't going to lie there and let Rapper shoot him, that was for sure.

As Rapper's steps approached, Rhodes lurched to his knees, then threw himself forward at what he hoped would be Rapper's softly bulging midsection. He was off, but not too far, and he had managed to take Rapper by surprise. His head hit Rapper in the side and staggered him backward.

Rhodes tried to gain his feet, but Nellie landed in the middle of his back. Rhodes rolled over, but that didn't help. Now Nellie was beneath him, but he had a strong grip around Rhodes's chest and was squeezing.

Rhodes rolled over again. Now Nellie was on top. No advantage there, either, except that Rapper, who was now on his feet, couldn't shoot for fear of hitting Nellie.

"Get off him, Nellie!" Rapper screamed, the thin edge of dementia in his voice. "Get off, or I'll shoot you too!"

Nellie tried to get up and Rhodes followed along, running backward with Nellie, who was trying to get away. Rhodes dug his feet into the ground, driving backward as hard as he could. Nellie, caught up in the rush, went along.

Things came to a sudden stop when they hit a tree. All the air went out of Nellie, and Rhodes tried to keep his balance.

Rapper fired the pistol, but the shot went wild in the darkness. So did the second one.

Rhodes tried to find cover. He got behind a tree trunk that wasn't quite thick enough and tried to think of what to do next. Pain was shooting up and down his arms and pulsing in his head.

A shot thudded into the tree trunk. Rapper was getting better in the dark, or luckier.

Then suddenly, as if it were right on him, Rhodes heard the wail of a siren. Headlights flooded through the trees, and there was the flashing of a light bar.

114

"Freeze, sucker!" It was Ruth Grady.

Quite a few things happened then, and Rhodes never remembered if they happened in any particular order or if they all happened at once.

No one froze. Rapper whirled around and fired two shots at the lights. Rhodes heard glass shatter. Ruth Grady began firing at the muzzle flashes. Nellie got up. Rhodes hit the dirt. There were more shots. Rhodes heard the motorcycles start and speed away.

Then Ruth was kneeling by him. "Got the keys to these cuffs, Sheriff?"

"Right pocket," Rhodes said, rolling into a position where she could reach them. She took them off, and Rhodes rubbed his wrists as he sat up.

"Too many trees," Ruth said. "I don't think I hit anybody. Should we go after them?"

"Not much chance of catching them," Rhodes said. "How many were there?"

"Three. One in the tent."

"Thought there had to be another one." Rhodes winced as the blood began to flow freely in his arms and hands once again, sending needles into his skin. "I'd like to say I had 'em where I wanted 'em, but you'd probably see right through that, wouldn't you."

Ruth laughed. "Probably."

"How'd you happen to show up here, anyway?"

"Hack called me, said you might need some backup."

"Hack's beginning to exceed his authority," Rhodes said. "All the same, I don't think I'll call him down for it this time." He stood up. "How much damage to the car?"

"Smashed a headlight, I think."

"I hope that's all," Rhodes said. "I'm beginning to feel like a one-man disaster area. Let's us get on back to town while I can still walk."

As they walked to the car, Rhodes saw that one of the

low-beam lights was out. There didn't seem to be much damage, otherwise. He got in and called Hack, telling him to send Buddy out to go over the tent and surrounding area. He didn't think there'd be anything to find, but he didn't want to pass up the chance.

The next morning Rhodes was very stiff and very sore. Muscles that he hadn't been aware of in the past now ached and throbbed. Muscles that he *had* been aware of hurt even more. He sat in his kitchen, drinking a Dr Pepper and thinking dark thoughts. Then he fed Speedo. He hadn't stopped and bought any dog food the night before, so he opened a can of Vienna sausage.

Speedo didn't look too happy about it. "Look, dog, if it's good enough for me, it's good enough for you," Rhodes said. Speedo nosed the lump of sausages around, then gave in and took the whole mass in one bite. He chewed around on it for a minute, swallowed, and then looked expectantly at Rhodes. "That's it," Rhodes said. "Behave youself and I'll get you something later. Go lie down somewhere."

Speedo didn't move, so Rhodes went back into the house and got dressed.

On the way to the jail, he stopped at Wal-Mart and bought a fifty-pound sack of Old Roy dog food. "It's the dry stuff from now on," he said aloud as he dumped the sack into the back of the pickup with a dull thud. "No more gourmet meals."

Hack was waiting eagerly as Rhodes walked into the jail, with a look on his face not unlike the one Speedo had worn earlier.

Rhodes didn't say a word. We'll see how he likes having to drag it out of me, Rhodes thought. Then he immediately relented.

"What do you want to hear?" he asked.

"About how you had 'em buffaloed," Hack said. "About how you had 'em where you wanted 'em."

"You've been talking to Ruth already," Rhodes said.

Hack laughed. "Ain't that girl a scutter? How many shots she get off?"

"I didn't count," Rhodes said honestly.

"She's a scutter," Hack repeated, shaking his head in appreciation. "Why, I bet if she didn't have to stop and help you up, she'd of rounded up the whole bunch."

"I wouldn't be surprised," Rhodes said. He laughed too, but not for the same reason as Hack. He was laughing because he figured Ruth's role as "the new deputy" was over. "Anything else?"

"Yeah, as a matter of fact there is," Hack said. "Two guys want to talk to you. They went over to the motel to have breakfast, but they'll be back pretty quick."

"What two guys?"

"Well, they're wearin' navy blue suits and burgundy ties. They got on thin gold watches with gold bands. And they got white shirts and black shoes that lace up and tie."

"We all know what that means," Rhodes said.

"That's right," Hack said. "Either you got business with two bankers from Houston or the federal boys are in town."

"How much would you bet that they're not bankers from Houston?" Rhodes asked.

"Not a whole hell of a lot," Hack said.

"Me either. I guess they didn't happen to mention what they wanted?"

"Sure they did. They wanted to talk to you."

"They probably need financial advice," Rhodes said.

"Probably," Hack said. "You goin' to talk to them?"

Rhodes went over and sat in his chair that no longer squeaked. "I don't expect I'll have too much choice. How long have they been gone?"

"Long enough to go through the Breakfast Special. They ought to be back before long."

"I can wait," Rhodes said. "Did Buddy come up with anything last night?"

"Got the tent and a couple of sleepin' rolls. Not much else. Said he'd go back out today when he could see and take another look."

Rhodes didn't think there would be anything. Rapper and Nellie probably traveled light. He thought about what had happened and what it meant. He didn't have much doubt about who the third person was. It had to be Wyneva. And it had to have been the third person who hit him in the head. Wyneva again.

Knowing *who,* or at least thinking that he knew who, didn't help Rhodes much with the *why.* There was obviously something going on, and he even thought that he knew a little about it, but he was missing too much. Maybe when he questioned Jayse and the other man, he'd find out something that would fill in the missing spaces in his thinking. Or maybe the two men in the navy blue suits would help him out. He wasn't betting too heavily on either pair, however.

Two men were dead, and Rhodes himself had taken a considerable beating. He didn't mind the latter too much, or he wouldn't have minded if it had led to anything on the murders, but he wasn't making enough progress. He began to get impatient for the blue suits to show up.

He didn't have to wait long. They came in the door of the jail, one behind the other, dressed exactly as Hack had described them. One was tall, nearly six feet, and the other was slightly taller, maybe six-two. They had short hair, and their eyes were alert. They said hello to Hack and shook hands with Rhodes.

"How about that Breakfast Special?" Hack asked, as they sat in the hard wooden chairs.

"I don't think I ever saw so much eggs and sausage in one place," the taller of the men said. His voice was deep and pleasant. He reached inside his jacket and took out his identification. "Roger Malvin," he said. "DEA. The gentleman with me is Robert Cox." His accent, obviously acquired in New York, sounded foreign in the jail.

Cox showed his own ID. "Pleased to meet you, Sheriff," he said. His accent was softer, nearer to Virginia than Malvin's.

"What can I do for you fellas?" Rhodes asked. He always felt his Texas drawl get broader and twangier when he talked to anyone from north of Oklahoma.

"We understand that you have two prisoners in the hospital," Malvin said. He was obviously the spokesman. "We would like for you to allow us to question them."

Rhodes looked over at Hack, who busied himself with some papers, probably blank, on the radio table. Sometimes Hack talked too much to strangers, even if he was sure they were federal agents. "What is it you want to talk to them about?"

It was Malvin's turn to look, and he looked at Cox, who shook his head slightly. "About a man named Buster Cullens," he said.

Rhodes thought for a second. He was willing to help the men out, but he wasn't going to do it for nothing.

"We could question them without your permission," Malvin said. "We're just trying to be cooperative."

Rhodes thought Malvin was being a little pushy. "I might have a guard on them," he said. "He might not let you in."

"I could get a court order," Malvin said, his voice no longer very pleasant.

"Maybe," Rhodes said. "Or maybe I know the judge better than you do."

"Just a minute," Cox said mildly. "We don't have to

argue about this. Surely you realize the importance of a federal investigation, Sheriff."

"I surely do," Rhodes said. "But I have my own priorities. These two men are involved in a murder. Maybe in two murders. I haven't questioned them yet myself."

"Of course we would want you to be present during any interrogation," Cox said.

Then Rhodes caught on. I must be getting old, he thought, to let them pull the old Mutt and Jeff on me. "I'll tell you what," he said. "I'll let you go over to the hospital with me and be present at *my* interrogation. How's that?"

The men looked at one another.

"There's a catch, though," Rhodes said before they could answer.

"What's the catch?" Malvin asked.

"You tell me what you know about these men, why you want to talk to them, and what you know about Buster Cullens. All of it. Otherwise, you can forget it. Go back to Washington, or wherever it is you come from, and leave the small-town crimes to the small-town boys."

Cox laughed. "We didn't mean to get you so upset, Sheriff. Maybe we'd better start over and see if we can't get off on a better footing."

"That's all right with me," Rhodes said.

"Good," said Malvin, his voice pleasant once more. "You're probably not going to like everything we have to say, however."

"I haven't liked much of it so far, anyway," Rhodes said. "So you might as well give me a try on the rest of it."

"Well, it's this way," Malvin said. "Cullens was one of ours."

Rhodes tried not to let his surprise show, but this was

120

one thing he hadn't taken into account. Then he realized that this was one of the things that he wasn't supposed to like. And he didn't. "You mean you sent a man into my county to do some sort of investigation and you didn't tell me? That's a little bit insulting."

"It wasn't meant to be," Cox said. "We were pretty sure we could trust you. Your record is as clean as any I've ever seen. But when it comes to dope, you never know who you can trust."

"I figured there was dope mixed up in this," Rhodes said. "I'm just not sure how."

"That's where we can help you out," Cox said.

"Yes," Malvin said. "Have you ever flown over this county in a helicopter?"

Rhodes was tempted to say that he flew around in helicopters all the time, but he restrained himself. "No," he said.

"Well, we have," Malvin said. "You'd be surprised what you can see when you do. Later we may give you a little ride."

"We got started on this because of some information we picked up from informants in an investigation of Los Muertos," Cox said. "We've learned a lot about them and their sources of dope."

"OK," Rhodes said. "I know that Bert Ramsey had a lot of money that he shouldn't have had. I've got some of it in my safe, and even more of it is tied up in television sets and microwaves. I just don't see how he was involved with dope, either as a source or as a consumer."

"He was growing it," Malvin said.

Rhodes was surprised again. "Where?"

"On his farm," Cox said.

Rhodes shook his head. "I've been there," he said. "It's right on the road. Anybody can see there's nothing growing there except grass and a few weeds. Besides, it's been too dry here to grow anything."

"That's why you need a little helicopter ride," Malvin said. "You know those woods on Ramsey's place?"

"Yes," Rhodes said.

"They aren't woods," Malvin said. "At least not much. Ramsey cleared them out. There's a row or two of trees, but inside that row there's a nice field of marijuana, irrigated out of a stock tank."

Rhodes knew that it must be true, but it was still hard to believe. "We'll have to harvest that marijuana and burn it," he said.

"Of course," Cox said. "But there's another little matter, don't forget. We've got a dead agent to account for."

"I think I might be able to help you on that one," Rhodes said.

14

RHODES HAD NEVER been in a helicopter before. What really amazed him was the noise. Whenever Malvin had anything to say, he had to put his head right next to Rhodes's ear and speak very loudly, almost in a shout. Cox had stayed behind. The pilot hadn't been introduced.

They had had to drive over to the next county to get the chopper, which was being looked after at the National Guard headquarters there. "It's not that we didn't trust you," Cox said as they drove over in the navy blue car that matched the navy blue suits. "It's just that we had to be sure. You know how it is . . . you find a huge marijuana field growing in a man's backyard, so to speak, and you have to wonder if he knows something about it."

"No," Rhodes said, "I don't know." And it was the truth. Rhodes knew himself, knew that he would never have dreamed of cashing in on something like marijuana, knew that such a thing would have been impossible for him. And nearly anyone who knew him knew that about him. Of course, he would have thought that it would have been impossible for Bert Ramsey to grow and sell dope, too.

"No hard feelings, I hope," Cox said. "After Ramsey was killed and you started questioning Cullens, he was convinced you were straight."

"Sometimes it's hard for us to trust anyone," Malvin said from the back seat. "Sometimes we don't even trust each other."

"Which brings us to Wyneva Greer," Cox said. He steered the car along at exactly the legal limit. He even wore his seat belt and shoulder harness, as required by law.

"How does that bring us to her?" Rhodes asked.

"It's a matter of trust," Malvin said. "We sent Cullens up here not long after we made a flyover of the county. He had a good cover. We arranged for him to live in a house on land owned by someone supposed to be his cousin, and anyone checking with the cousin would get the same story. So what was he doing with Wyneva Greer? How come he's dead?"

"He was living with Wyneva, that's for sure," Rhodes said. "But that's all that's sure. Why he was living with her, whether it was his idea or hers, that's something we'll have to find out. When I walked into that house, Rapper and his goons were there, and one of them had an axe handle. We'll know more about that when we hear what killed Cullens."

"Maybe we should have stopped by that hospital before we did this flyover," Malvin said.

"Rhodes needs to see this," Cox said. "Those guys will keep."

Rhodes had made sure they would keep. He had called Ruth Grady from the jail and put her on guard at their adjoining rooms, not that he was really worried. Any stranger would have been noticed and called down immediately in the Clearview Hospital, especially a stranger that looked like Rapper or Nellie. Besides, Rhodes wasn't at all sure there was any urgency about talking to the two men. They weren't the type to tell their life stories at the drop of a hat.

"If those men don't talk, then what?" Malvin asked, echoing Rhodes's thoughts.

"I don't know," Rhodes told him. "It may be that

Rapper and Nellie have split the scene entirely. They could be in Houston by now, for all we know.

"But you don't really think that," Cox said.

"No," Rhodes said. "I don't. I think they're still around. I'm not sure why, but I think they're still around."

"It's either the dope or the money," Cox said. "You can bet on that."

"Could be," Rhodes said. "But you haven't had any run-ins with Rapper. I have. I think he's crazy. Oh, maybe not crazy enough to be put away, but bad enough."

"How bad is that?" Malvin asked.

"Bad enough to stay around just because he wants to get back at me," Rhodes said. "I've messed his playhouse up. If you could have seen the way he acts, you'd know what I mean."

"I guess that's another one of those things we'll find out about later on," Cox said.

It wasn't a particularly comforting thought.

While the pilot warmed up the helicopter, Rhodes stood by the car and looked at it. Cox had called it a Jet Ranger, but he had assured Rhodes that it wasn't jet propelled. "Carries four people in comfort," Cox said. "Comfort's relative, of course. Anyway, it's just right for the kind of jobs we do." Even as far away as they stood, he had to raise his voice almost to a yell for Rhodes to hear him.

Then Malvin tugged at Rhodes's arm and they went to get on board. They bent from the waist as they passed under the whickering blades. Rhodes wasn't sure just how tall he was, or just how high the blades were, but he'd seen people on TV duck when they went under them, and he wasn't going to take any chances.

There was hardly any wind at all, and the lift-off was

smooth and effortless. Rhodes had carefully strapped himself in, but the open sides still gave him a distinct feeling of discomfort.

The feeling soon wore off, however, as Rhodes was caught up in the new view he had of Blacklin County. This was nothing like flying in a plane; they seemed so close to the ground that it was almost as if they could jump down.

"Give him the scenic route," Malvin yelled to the pilot, and that's what they got.

They went over the courthouse and jail, and Rhodes was even able to pick out his own house.

"You'd be surprised at how some people keep their backyards," Malvin said in Rhodes's ear, and it was true. Protected from everyone's eyes by wood fences, the backyards of some homes were littered with everything from old, rusting auto bodies to broken toilets. Some of the homes that had immaculate front yards might have a backyard that looked like a dog run, or was filled with piles of trash consisting of everything from bathtubs to oil drums. It all surprised Rhodes a little, but at least it made him feel better about his own backyard.

Then they were out of Eller's Prairie. As they coasted past Bert Ramsey's house, Rhodes noted the tops of the trees that formed the line at the back of the property. They gained a little altitude, and he could see where the trees had been cleared out. Then he could see into a clearing, where the marijuana plants were growing.

They circled around three times. After Rhodes had seen enough, they headed back to the National Guard Armory.

"You guys take cruises like that often?" Rhodes asked Malvin after they were back on the ground.

"Often enough," Malvin said. "You'd be surprised at

the stuff we find growing around in clearings just like that one at Ramsey's place."

Rhodes would have been surprised once, but not any more. If dope was growing in Blacklin County, it could be anywhere. He thought about it all the way to the hospital.

The Clearview Hospital was small and old, but it had been kept up well and served the needs of the county. Most patients requiring any kind of specialized care or treatment went to Dallas or Houston, and the residents of Blacklin County felt lucky to have any kind of hospital at all. It wasn't as hard now for Clearview to attract young doctors as it had been a few years earlier, so the hospital was more than adequately staffed.

It was not especially designed for security, but anyone entering one of its three wings had to pass by the front desk, unless he took the emergency room entrance or the service entrance. He would be noticed immediately in any case, and if he looked suspicious he would be in trouble. Rhodes figured that Rapper would look suspicious even if he tried a disguise.

Jayse and the other man were in adjoining rooms at the end of a hall. Ruth Grady sat on a chair between the two closed doors. She stood up when she saw Rhodes and the federal men coming. Rhodes made the introductions, all the time thinking about the smell. Hospitals all smelled the same, no matter whether they were small or large, and it was a smell that Rhodes always associated with unpleasant memories. He had done so even before the death of his wife, but now the smell would always remind him of death. He wondered how many people felt that way, and thought that it was no real surprise that so many people feared hospitals.

Ruth stayed in the hall while Rhodes and the federal men went into the room. Jayse lay in the bed, his leg in a cast. The county hadn't sprung for a TV set, so he was looking vacantly at the ceiling. The room contained an uncomfortable-looking chrome chair with a vinyl-covered seat and back, a nightstand, and the inevitable shelf-on-wheels device that served as a table. The walls were a pale institutional green. Rhodes was glad he didn't have to stay there, and he wondered if Jayse might not prefer the jail.

"Well, Jayse," Rhodes said, "it looks like you're in for some trouble." He introduced Malvin and Cox. "These fellas can get you put away for a long time. Me, I'm just a small-town sheriff who can probably get you for murder. These guys are going to get you for the murder of a federal agent."

"I didn't kill nobody," Jayse said. "I don't know what you're talking about. What federal agent?" Jayse was a bad liar. His voice quavered, and he refused to look at anyone in the room, keeping his eyes on the pale green ceiling.

"Look," Malvin said, "we know it looks bad for you, you being found with the axe handle. It's really too bad, but we know from the autopsy that Cullens was killed with blows from a blunt instrument. Some of the bruises match that axe handle exactly. But maybe you didn't do it. Maybe you just picked up the handle. Maybe someone else did the dirty work." Malvin was a much better liar that Jayse. They hadn't even checked the autopsy report. But Malvin's voice never wavered from the calm, matter-of-fact tone in which he began talking.

It was quite cool in the room. In fact, it was too cool. Rhodes had never been in a hospital room that was warm, as far as he could remember. Still, Jayse was sweating. He wiped his upper lip. "I didn't kill nobody," he said. "You're right about the handle. I just picked it up. We thought the sheriff here was the killer comin' back, so I hid to get him."

"Now that just won't do, Jayse," Rhodes said. "I called out before I came in. I even said Rapper's name."

Jayse shook his head. "Don't matter. You didn't say you were the law, did you?"

Rhodes wasn't sure, but he didn't recall identifying himself. "I don't remember," he said.

"Well, you didn't," Jayse said. "So we couldn't be sure who you were. You might've been the killer, come back for us."

"But you had the axe handle, Jayse," Rhodes said. "What could I have killed you with?"

"How do I know? Maybe you had a rocket launcher." Jayse was getting cocky now. Rhodes had seen it happen before. A man would try his story out, afraid of being caught in the lie. But when it couldn't be contradicted, he'd relax and stick to it until hell froze over. Jayse was that way.

Malvin and Cox tried. Rhodes helped all he could. But Jayse just stuck to his story. Rhodes wondered if it would work with a jury. It might. It just might.

The other man, whose name turned out to be Ted Barrett, was sullen and withdrawn. He was, if anything, less helpful than Jayse, because he simply refused to talk at all. He answered only with grunts and head shakes— very small shakes, since he was still suffering from a concussion.

Back in the hall, Cox shook his head, too, more vehemently than Barrett had. "Damn! Those two are bound to know something. There've got to be better ways to get it out of them."

"They'll be a lot less comfortable when they get to the jail," Malvin said. "How long will that be, Sheriff?"

"Whenever the doctor releases them," Rhodes said. "That might be a while, though." He turned to Ruth Grady. "Could you drop a word with that informant of yours?"

"I imagine so," she said. "When?"

"The sooner the better," Rhodes said. "Just mention that you've been guarding Jayse and Ted, and say that they've talked. You don't have to be too specific. Just let the word get out that we're satisfied with what we've heard. Stress the federal involvement."

"I can do that tonight," Ruth said.

Cox and Malvin weren't too happy, but they had to be satisfied. It was the best they could do until either they had some solid evidence or they got hold of Rapper. They drove Rhodes back to the jail and dropped him off.

Lawton and Hack were having a laugh when Rhodes came inside, but they stifled it long enough to say that Dr. Sam White had called. Cullens had died just about exactly as Malvin had described it—several blows from a blunt instrument, probably the axe handle. The blow that had killed him was a particularly strong one to the back of the head.

"I don't guess you two were laughing at a man being killed like that," Rhodes said.

"You know us better than that, Sheriff," Lawton said. He looked a little disappointed that the thought would ever have crossed Rhodes's mind. "It was something else entirely."

"I see," Rhodes said, and waited. He knew that he was being set up again, and that it would be Hack's job to finish the story. "What's happened."

"Old Lady Laughlin's been arrested," Hack said.

Rhodes looked at both men sternly. There was such a thing as carrying a joke too far. "In the first place," he said, " 'Old Lady Laughlin' isn't as old as either one of you."

Neither man looked ashamed. "Don't matter," Hack said. "That's what ever'body calls her."

"You're talking about the president of the historical

society, one of the best schoolteachers this town's ever had, right?" Rhodes said.

"That's the one," Lawton said.

"The woman my daughter thought was about the only saving grace of the Clearview Independent School District?"

"You got it," Lawton said.

"I just don't believe it," Rhodes said. "What's the charge?"

"Squeezin' the Charmin," Hack said. Both he and Lawton broke into laughter.

Rhodes just looked at them until they stopped. "I can't believe this," he said. "Have you two been sniffing glue?"

Hack tried to look serious. "Swear to God, Sheriff. It's the truth." He put his hand over his heart.

"*Squeezing the Charmin?*"

"Over to the Safeway," Lawton said helpfully.

"The manager called it in," Hack said. "He caught 'er in the act. I sent Buddy right on over. He's the one wrote the ticket. Ask him if you don't believe me." He crossed his arms and looked righteous.

"All right, I guess I believe you. But there must be more to it than that," Rhodes said.

"Nope," Hack said. "That's it . . . well, that's most of it."

"I thought so," Rhodes said. "Let's have *all* of it."

"Well, the manager saw her. She was squeezin' the Charmin, just like I said. Or at least that's what it looked like she was doin' at first. Now that's all right, the manager said. They see those ads on the TV and they just can't resist. Nothin' like a little advertisin' to get folks' attention. But then she just kept it up. Seemed like she was really gettin' into it. When she finally stopped, he went to check it out. Seems like she'd ripped the label off the package, needed it for some kind of mail-in refund or somethin'. He figured that was theft. She was still in the store when Buddy got there."

"He didn't write her a ticket for theft," Rhodes said. "I guess he has a little sense."

"Nope," Hack said. "I mean 'nope' he didn't write her a ticket for theft, not that he doesn't have a little sense. He gave her a ticket for criminal mischief. Maybe he threw in a little trespassin'. I'm not sure about that one. Anyway, the manager don't want her back in there, least not for a while."

Rhodes wasn't really surprised. People would do strange things to save a dollar, or even less. He was sorry that it had to be Mrs. Laughlin, though, and he knew that although the incident was funny to Lawton and Hack, it wasn't funny to her. It was very probably the worst thing she'd ever done in her life. She would pay her fine and worry about it for years. Meanwhile, Rapper and Nellie were out scot-free. Some days really got a man down, and it looked as if this was going to be one of those days.

Rhodes told Hack to take care of things, got in his pickup, and went home for lunch.

15

RHODES THOUGHT THAT his house had never seemed quite so empty. It was one of those times when he almost wished that Ralph Claymore had won the primary election, one of those times when being sheriff seemed to be a job that someone else could do better.

It wasn't just the empty house—Rhodes had gotten nearly used to that, though that was probably part of it. It was mainly the fact that he couldn't quite get a handle on what was happening. Rapper had gotten away from him twice, and unless Jayse talked, the chances for finding Rapper again looked dim. There was a chance that Ruth Grady's contact would get Rapper the word that Jayse had talked and thus smoke Rapper out, but Rhodes couldn't count on that.

To top it all off, there wasn't even any bologna for a sandwich. Rhodes wondered briefly just how many bologna sandwiches he'd eaten since Claire's death, but it wasn't something that he wanted to think about for too long. He wondered if Ivy liked bologna. He needed to talk to her, having failed to call her last night. After his tussle with Rapper, he hadn't felt like talking to anyone.

At least he had something for Speedo to eat. He went outside and got the sack of Old Roy out of the pickup and carried it into the backyard. Speedo was there, sleeping in the shade of a native pecan tree. He heard the crackling of the dog food sack, or maybe Rhodes's footsteps, and raised his head.

Rhodes put down the sack and went into the house to

look for a bowl. He found an old Tupperware salad bowl in one of the cabinets and brought it out. Then he ripped the top off the bag of dog food. Speedo's ears perked up at the ripping sound. He got to his feet, shook himself, and trotted over to Rhodes.

Rhodes poured some of the food into the bowl. He had intended to carry it over to the shade, but Speedo immediately poked his nose in and started eating. Rhodes set the dog food bag in the garage and rummaged around until he found an old watering dish. He filled it at a faucet and set it by the food. Speedo stopped eating and slurped the water noisily.

"Sorry I forgot about the water," Rhodes said. "It's been a while since I had a dog."

Speedo didn't seem to mind. He finished drinking, then turned back to the food. Rhodes stood watching him eat. The day had gotten hot, and Rhodes could feel the heat soaking through his clothes. A droplet of sweat ran down his ribs.

"You had the right idea, staying in the shade," he said to the dog. "You go on and eat. I'm going back in."

Talking to Speedo had cheered Rhodes up some, but not enough. He didn't even feel like watching the *Million Dollar Movie,* a Hammer gem called *Prehistoric Women.* Any other day he would have watched it with amazement, but he had too much on his mind to be amazed or amused by an inept movie.

Who killed Bert Ramsey? Rapper? Why? The crop hadn't been harvested, and Ramsey was growing more all the time. To kill him was to cut off the source. Cullens? Surely not. A government agent wanted information, not a man's death. Wyneva Greer? She hadn't even been living with Ramsey for months. Yet Rhodes felt that they were all somehow involved.

As for Cullens, Rapper could easily have tortured him for information and killed him either by accident or design. Or he could have watched cheerfully while one of the others tortured him. Rapper was that kind of man. The best thing that Rhodes could say for Rapper was that he'd never seen either Rapper or one of the others with a gun.

And that was another thing that really bothered Rhodes. He hadn't found his own pistol the night before, and neither had anyone else. Rhodes had another pistol, and he was wearing it, but now he was pretty sure that Rapper had a pistol, too. That didn't cheer Rhodes up at all.

He stepped outside and looked in the flat, black mailbox, remembering that he hadn't checked the day before. There was a circular advertising a sale at Wal-Mart, and another circular offering him siding for his house ABSO-LUTELY FREE!!!!! if he would consent to being a "Showcase Home." He decided to decline. There was also an envelope with a cartoon drawing of Ed McMahon on the outside, promising to Mr. Dan Rhodes that he had (if he was lucky) a prize of 10 MILLION DOLLARS!!!!! awaiting him. Rhodes put that envelope carefully aside. He always responded to sweepstakes letters, even though he never bought any of the products and figured that his chances of winning were nil. He also figured that the 22 cents he spent on the stamp was a small price to pay for the ten or fifteen minutes of pleasure he got from thinking about what he would do with TEN MILLION DOLLARS!!!!!

The last item was a letter from Kathy, written on some kind of card that folded into its own envelope and sealed with a gold foil circle. He peeled off the circle and read the neatly penned letter.

Kathy had settled in to her new apartment, and while she hadn't really met anyone yet, she was sure she was going to like it. She missed her father, of course, and she hoped that he was eating something besides bologna sandwiches for lunch. Rhodes laughed. So far he hadn't eaten anything.

Kathy went on to say that she hoped Ivy was doing well, and she wondered if he had any news for her about himself and Ivy. Rhodes knew that she strongly approved of the idea of his getting married again, and he knew that he should write her and let her know of the recent developments. He wasn't much on writing. Maybe he could call.

Then he thought about the "recent developments," something he hadn't really allowed himself to do. He still wasn't able to devote his full attention to the matter, but he decided to think about it anyway.

Except that he still didn't know what to think.

On the one hand, there was obviously strong feeling between himself and Ivy Daniel. He liked to be with her, and he could tell that she enjoyed herself in his company. And, of course, there was something more than that, as he'd discovered a couple of nights ago. Not that things had gotten out of hand. Far from it. But still, they had kissed, and there was certainly an electricity in it that he'd been pretty sure that he'd never feel again. He was too old for that sort of thing. But there it was. To tell the truth, it scared him a little.

On the other hand, there was his job, which Ivy had at least once expressed a concern about. It could certainly be dangerous, though it usually wasn't. It usually wasn't even as physically taxing as it had been for the last few days. It did demand that he be on call twenty-four hours a day, just like a doctor. If something came up that required the presence of the chief law officer of the county, he had to appear, no matter if it was three o'clock in the morning or the middle of Sunday afternoon.

And on the other hand—if I *had* another hand, Rhodes thought—there was Ivy herself. She had run for justice of the peace once and might want to again. But if she

136

married Rhodes, that would be impossible. Definite conflict of interest, there.

Of course, Rhodes thought, he had more or less proposed to Ivy, and she had more or less accepted. He wished he could remember the exact words, but he couldn't. Not that he was trying to weasel out of it. In fact, sitting there in the empty house, nobody there but him and the dog, the idea of Ivy being around pleased him quite a bit. She wouldn't be there during the day, naturally, since she would want to keep her job, but just the thought of her presence would cheer him up.

He wondered if Bert Ramsey had felt that way about Wyneva Greer, or if Buster Cullens had. The more he thought about Buster Cullens, the more he wondered about Wyneva Greer. There really wasn't much doubt in his mind that Wyneva had been the third person in the woods at Rapper's tent, though he hadn't mentioned that to Malvin and Cox. Could it be that they knew something that they hadn't mentioned to him?

Maybe he was getting cynical. Surely two federal agents, who had decided to be so frank with him about how they hadn't quite trusted him, were going to level now, weren't they? Probably not.

They had said that they wanted to know why Wyneva was with Buster, but maybe they knew. Maybe they just didn't want Rhodes to know that they knew. Maybe they didn't want *Rhodes* to know.

When you looked at it, Rhodes thought, it was really pretty obvious. Buster Cullens knew about Bert Ramsey. He didn't know everything, though. He didn't know where the dope was going after it was harvested. So he stole Ramsey's girl and found out from her. Or he tried to find out.

Maybe he made a mistake, slipped up, was too obvious, and Wyneva had caught on. And instead of reporting to Ramsey—after all, she'd left him already—she'd reported to Rapper. Rapper had done the rest, after first trying to find out how much Cullens knew, and after killing Bert Ramsey to shut his mouth permanently. Now there was no one left to tie Rapper and Los Muertos into the dope. It was just there in Ramsey's backyard, so to speak, with no one to blame except a dead man. And if the federal boys hadn't come by, Rapper could have harvested it with no one the wiser.

All in all, Rhodes thought, it wasn't a bad theory. There were a few holes in it, though. For one thing, it seemed to Rhodes that Rapper, though obviously a lunatic, was fairly clever. He would certainly realize that it was much better to be brought in on a dope rap than on a double homicide.

But connecting Rapper to Ramsey's death would not be easy, and it was only an accident that Rhodes had walked in on Rapper at Cullens's house. It wasn't Rapper's fault that Rhodes had been able to walk out of the latter situation. So maybe it was the way Rhodes had it figured. He thought he would play it that way and see what happened, anyway.

He walked over to the phone and called the Trail's End motel. "Hey, Gerald," he said when the desk clerk answered. "You got two guys named Cox and Malvin registered?"

"Sure do, Sheriff," Gerald answered.

Rhodes was a little surprised that they'd used their real names, but since Cullens was dead and probably exposed anyway, he guessed it didn't really matter. Besides, he didn't know how the federal boys preferred to operate, anyway. "Connect me with their room, will you?" he asked.

"Sure thing, Sheriff." Rhodes heard clicking sounds and then the ringing of the telephone.

Cox answered. "Hello?"

"It's Dan Rhodes. I've got one little question for you."

"Shoot," Cox said. "Figuratively speaking, of course."

"It's about Wyneva Greer."

"What about her?" Cox said. No hesitation. No wariness.

"I just have this feeling you know more than you're telling," Rhodes said.

The line hummed for a second or two while Cox said nothing. Then there was a sigh. "What makes you think that?"

"It's just a feeling I have," Rhodes said. "Plus the fact that I just don't really believe that an agent of yours could live with someone for months without you knowing quite a bit about what was going on."

"Is this telephone secure?"

Rhodes laughed. Cox had asked in all seriousness, but Rhodes found it hard to take the question in the spirit in which it had been intended. The idea of a bugged telephone in Blacklin County was almost ridiculous. "It's secure," he said.

"I guess it may seem pretty funny that I'd even ask," Cox said. "Just a habit. Anyway, you're right. Another little habit we have is holding back a little something. No reflection on you."

"Of course not," Rhodes said, not believing a word of it.

"We did have a little information on the Greer woman," Cox said. "Cullens had evidently met her at some kind of nightclub while she was with Ramsey. So he decided to get to know her a little better, hoping for some inside information. He got to know her a little better than he intended." There was a note of disapproval in the voice now. "Cullens had been in a little trouble for things like that in the past."

"Did he learn anything?"

"Not enough," Cox said. "She was tied in with Los Muertos, that's definite. She apparently came to the area to find out where Bert Ramsey was and what he was doing. We believe Los Muertos, or at least Rapper, planned to use him in the dope business, which seems to be what happened."

"Once a dead man, always a dead man," Rhodes said.

"What?"

"Never mind. That's pretty much the way I had it figured," Rhodes said. "Is it possible at all that Cullens made a mistake in dealing with her? That he maybe gave too much away?"

"It's possible," Cox said, the disapproval strong in his voice now. "I was against his being assigned to this job. I didn't like to work with him. He was undependable."

"Well, you won't have to worry about that anymore," Rhodes said.

"True," Cox said with no apparent regret. "Anything else?"

"Not at the moment," Rhodes said. "If I think of something, I'll give you a call." He hung up the phone.

He wished he knew more about Wyneva Greer, and he thought back to the only two times he had seen her. Both times, she had looked afraid. Not that he blamed her for looking that way at the funeral. Mrs. Ramsey was a formidable woman, and even Rhodes might have given way had she been advancing on him. But not Wyneva. She might have looked a bit frightened, but she left only to avoid a scene.

What was it that Mrs. Ramsey had said to her? Rhodes tried to remember. Something like, "Bert wouldn't be here if it wasn't for you." He wondered if Mrs. Ramsey blamed Wyneva for the death, or if she even thought that Wyneva had something to do with it. Maybe Mrs. Ramsey knew more than he thought. He would have to talk to her again.

Wyneva hadn't spoken on Cullens's porch. Rhodes had thought at the time that she was afraid of Cullens, but it could have been that she was afraid of Rhodes, afraid that he was onto the game. Maybe even afraid that he had come to arrest her for the murder.

All of Rhodes's speculations, however, had led him nowhere. Oh, well, he thought, at least I've cleared the air. At least I have some idea of where I stand.

It was strange, but the quiet time of sitting and thinking through what he knew and didn't know had made him feel much better. If he still hadn't figured anything out, he at least knew where he stood. And what he didn't know, he'd thought about. There was the pretense of action, even if no action had been taken, even if no decisions had been made.

He looked at the clock. The whole afternoon had slipped by. Time had a way of doing that to him now, a sign of age, he guessed. It seemed as if the years went by like bullets. No wonder the young seemed to get more done. They had more time. When he was younger, the afternoon would have seemed to him like a week seemed now. There was a certain amount of unfairness there, but he didn't dwell on it.

He went back outside. Speedo was still under the tree, but he looked much more content. Rhodes picked up the water dish, and the sun-heated water sloshed out over his hand. "Sorry I forgot to put this in the shade," he said. He carried it and the food bowl over to the tree where Speedo lay. He got the dog food and poured a little more in the bowl, then refilled the water bowl. Speedo watched with a bit of interest, but he didn't stir himself to get up and eat or drink. There were times when Rhodes envied dogs. Speedo obviously didn't mind that Cullens was dead. He was getting food and water. He had a shady place to lie down. He had, in fact, just about everything he needed. If he couldn't be young again, Rhodes thought, he might like to be a dog.

Rhodes went back in the house and walked to the telephone, this time to call Ivy. She would be home from work now.

She answered on the first ring. "Hello?"

"It's me," Rhodes said. "Want to go to a funeral?"

16

THE CLEARVIEW CEMETERY had been located in the same spot ever since the first settler was buried there a little over a hundred years before. It had grown considerably since that first grave, but probably none of those who lay at rest there had ever been to a funeral quite like the one to which Rhodes was taking Ivy.

The cemetery was on the western edge of the town, surrounded by a low fence of iron spikes. There was a wrought iron arch over the main entrance, which was never closed. Every now and then Rhodes would send a patrol through late at night to run out the high school kids who had found it a quiet place to park.

There was not a lot of green grass on the graves; the recent rain hadn't been enough to help much. Rhodes drove through the entrance and down the winding gravel roads to the north end. There was no one else there yet.

Rhodes and Ivy got out of the pickup. Though it didn't appear to be so on the approaching drive, the cemetery was located on a hilltop. They could see the pasture land around them, down the slope. At the bottom of the slope and partway across a little valley there was a railroad track heading north and south.

The day had cooled off a little, and Rhodes liked standing there on the hill. There was a late afternoon breeze, and it was very quiet.

"I wonder if they can hear the trains," Ivy said, looking down at the tracks. "They have to whistle for the crossing, don't they?"

The nearest crossing was about a half mile away. "Sure they do," Rhodes said. "Did you ever hear a real train whistle?"

"You mean from a steam engine? I don't remember. I guess I must have, but if I did it was a long time ago," Ivy said.

"I heard lots of 'em," Rhodes said. "The house I grew up in was less than a mile from the tracks, nothing between the house and them but some mesquite trees. When I was a kid, I'd go to sleep at night listening for the whistle." He paused. "They can't hear it, I guess. If they could, the ones that've been here long enough would miss the real thing. Diesel's just not the same. Not very many of those even come through now, anyway." He shook his head and grinned. "I'm beginning to sound like the old-timer in a B western. How'd we get off on that?"

"I think the place we're in might've had something to do with it," Ivy said. "Did you really bring me up here for a funeral, or did you have something else in mind?" She stepped over to Rhodes and took his arm, pressing it against her plaid shirt.

Rhodes almost blushed, but not quite. "There's really going to be a funeral," he said. "If Ballinger doesn't show up, I'm going to bury *him*. He'll be here."

Sure enough, in a few minutes they saw Ballinger's hearse, or one of them, driving along the road. Rhodes hadn't really given the burial much thought, but trusted Ballinger to do it right, once he made up his mind to do it. Then Rhodes realized that there wasn't a grave.

The hearse stopped and Clyde Ballinger got out. He had been driving himself. There was another man inside, and Rhodes assumed there were others in the back.

"Where's the grave, Clyde?" Rhodes asked.

"Don't worry, Sheriff," Ballinger said. "It's dug and ready, back over behind the Walpole plot." He started walking, and Rhodes and Ivy followed.

143

The Walpole 'plot' was by far the most elaborate area in the cemetery, the Walpoles having gotten rich in oil and being able to afford pretty much what they wanted in the way of final resting places. The area occupied by the graves was semicircular, with the outside of the semicircle being surrounded by Greek columns spaced ten feet apart. Rhodes could never remember just what kind of columns they were, though he'd had to learn in school to distinguish among Doric, Ionic, and Corinthian. It wasn't the kind of knowledge that tended to stick with a person.

The various Walpoles were spaced around the area and located easily by the huge headstones, by a wide margin the largest and most elaborate and gaudy in the county. One was distinguished by five angels standing on it.

Ballinger cut right through the plot. The grass in this plot had been watered all through the dry summer, and there were several flower beds that gave evidence of careful tending. "Walpoles hire all that work done," Ballinger said, indicating the flower beds. "They have a man who comes out for a couple of hours twice a week."

At the back of the plot, at the apex of the semicircle, there was an archway, which Ballinger stepped through. It actually led nowhere, since the Walpoles had located their private burial area at the extreme north end of the cemetery. From this vantage point, Rhodes could see in the distance—about a quarter of a mile—the backs of the houses that faced a paved road leading from Clearview to a major highway. He could also see that there was an open grave.

"Is this legal?" Ivy asked.

"We have the sheriff with us, don't we?" Ballinger said.

"I think she means that it might not be strictly legal for a burial plot to be located right here," Rhodes said.

"I know that," Ballinger said. "Just a little funeral director's humor there. But it's legal, all right. Strictly speaking, I guess that we shouldn't be here, but I bought up this part of the cemetery years ago. It's part of the cemetery land, all right. It's just that the Walpole family didn't want anybody to be buried behind them. They wanted the prime spot, right at the end of the line. Except that you'll notice the land slopes down just a little bit, here, and they didn't want to be on that slope. With all the money they had, they should have bought this part if they didn't want company. But don't worry, we won't be putting up any headstones. We don't even have any heads." He laughed.

"More funeral director's humor?" Ivy asked.

Ballinger wasn't a bit bothered by her tone. "You might say so. I got one more. The Walpoles don't have to worry, because there won't be any *body* buried here. At least not this time." He laughed again.

Rhodes and Ivy didn't laugh. They looked around for the hearse, which was making its way to them, having gone around on the road as far as it could and then cut across the grass.

"You know," Ballinger said, shaking his head, "I'm a little disappointed that all these arms and legs didn't turn out to be part of a big case. I was reading a book the other day about this killer down in Houston, the Houston Hacker, they called him, and he was really a vicious guy—"

"I don't want to hear about him," Ivy said.

"Was this fact or fiction?" Rhodes said.

The hearse arrived, and Ballinger directed it to a stopping place. Then he came back to answer Rhodes. "Fiction," he said. "It had this weird cover on it, of a knife stabbing through a strawberry. Anyway—"

"Never mind," Rhodes said. If the Hacker wasn't real, he wasn't interested. For a minute there, he'd thought that there might be some far-fetched tie-in with Dr. Rawlings, but obviously there wasn't. All he wanted to do now was to get what was in the hearse under the ground and forget about it, even if he couldn't forget what had happened later.

The driver of the hearse got out and opened the back door. Two men who had been riding inside stepped down, and the driver helped them slide a wooden casket box out the back.

"Wood's all Rawlings left enough to pay for," Ballinger said.

"But that isn't even a coffin," Ivy said. "It's just a wooden box like they ship coffins in."

"*I* know that," Ballinger said. "I don't really think it'll make a difference to anything that's inside. You want to be the fourth pallbearer, Sheriff?"

"Why not?" Rhodes said. He stepped over to help the other three men unload the plain white wooden box. It really wasn't very heavy at all.

They carried it over and set it on the muddy earth piled beside the grave. One of the men went back to the hearse and came back with two long ropes, which he laid across the open grave.

"Nothing fancy here," Ballinger said, "but it'll get the job done."

Two of the men held the ends of the ropes while Rhodes and the other man maneuvered the box into place. Then the four of them lowered the box to its rest.

"Sheriff," Ballinger said, "do you think we ought to say any last words now?"

Ballinger had gotten awfully pious all of a sudden, Rhodes thought, but maybe it was only a natural reaction. "May they rest in peace," he said. A terrible pun about pieces occurred to him, but he suppressed it. Ballinger stood with his head bowed for a minute, then looked up.

"I guess that does it," Ballinger said. "Cover 'em up,

boys." The three men went to the hearse and came back with shovels. While Ballinger, Rhodes and Ivy watched, the men began shoveling in the dirt.

"Shouldn't take them too long," Ballinger said. "I hope you're satisfied with this, Sheriff."

Rhodes shook his head. "I guess so. This whole thing has been a real problem, and it's not one I'd like to have again. Who'd have guessed it would be so hard to get rid of a few legally amputated limbs?"

"The law's peculiar," Ballinger said. "You of all people ought to know that."

"I guess I should have checked to make sure everything was in that box," Rhodes said.

"Trust me, Sheriff," Ballinger said. "I wouldn't make a mistake about something like that."

"Then that's the end of that," Rhodes said. "Let's go, Ivy. See you later, Clyde."

Ballinger gave an idle wave as he watched the grave being filled in. Rhodes and Ivy cut back through the Walpole plot and walked to the pickup. The sun was going down, now, and there was a bright reddish glow in the western sky. The breeze felt almost cool, and except for a few insect sounds it was very quiet. Then, from far off to the north they heard a train whistle.

"I guess it might not be so bad to be buried here," Ivy said. "Even if you couldn't hear the train whistle."

Rhodes thought about Claire, who had been buried in her home town. "Let's not worry about that for a while," he said.

Ivy shivered slightly. "It was just a thought," she said. "How about some supper?"

"That's a better thought," Rhodes said. They got in the pickup and went to the Bluebonnet for a hamburger. They had left the Bluebonnet and were driving toward Ivy's house when Rhodes worked himself up to asking the question. "When do you think we ought to get married?"

Ivy laughed. Rhodes liked to hear it, even though he was pretty sure she was laughing at him. "I was beginning to wonder if you'd really asked me," she said. "Or if you'd remember."

"I wouldn't forget something like that," Rhodes said, trying not to sound defensive. "I've been pretty busy." He briefly brought her up to date on his activities.

"I just hope you're around long enough and stay in one piece long enough for us to have a wedding," Ivy said. "Not a very big one," she added after looking at Rhodes's face. "Just you and me and the justice of the peace would be fine. And Kathy, naturally."

"I wouldn't want to push you into something you didn't want," Rhodes said. "I mean. . . ."

"I know what you mean," Ivy said. "You mean you're really not sure about this. Well, I'm not either."

Rhodes started to say something, but she stopped him. "You're sure about the important things. So am I. But you're thinking about Claire and what happened to her, just like I think about Cal and what happened to him. I wouldn't want anything to happen to you. I wouldn't want to lose you, too."

Rhodes sighed and relaxed. Ivy had put into words the thoughts that had been running around in his head without expression for the last few days. He knew exactly what she meant, and more important, he knew for the first time exactly what he'd been thinking. Or trying to think about, and not succeeding.

"I don't want to do it right away," Ivy said. "We could both use a little more time to think, don't you agree?"

Rhodes nodded his head affirmatively.

"Good. How about December? I've always liked the Christmas season, and I'm sure we could both take a few days off around that time."

148

Rhodes started to tell her the Christmas season was definitely not a time of peace on earth, that in fact it was a time of high crime statistics, a time of shoplifting, theft, burglary, and sometimes even suicide. But he didn't. Instead, he said, "It sounds like a good idea to me."

17

BUDDY CAUGHT UP with Rhodes just as he and Ivy arrived at her house. Leaning out of the window of the county car, Buddy looked like anything but a deputy. He was thin and bony, with a head much too large for the broom-straw neck it sat on. His upper torso stuck so far out the window that Rhodes wondered how he was able to sit upright in the car seat when he pulled himself back in. His almost comical appearance sometimes fooled people. Buddy was a good lawman.

"Got a call from Hack," Buddy said. "He's tryin' to locate you."

"What's the message?" Rhodes asked.

"He says that Miz Ramsey telephoned a few minutes ago. She thinks someone's messin' around in Bert Ramsey's house. Says she saw lights movin' around in there. He thought you might want to be the one who goes out to check, seein' as how you've got a personal interest."

"He's right about that," Rhodes said.

"He said to tell you to take a backup this time."

Rhodes laughed. "I will. We'll go out together. Just give me a minute to see Ivy to the door." He and Ivy got out and walked to the house.

"Be careful," Ivy said.

"Don't worry," Rhodes told her. "Buddy can take care of me."

"Maybe," Ivy said, giving him a light kiss on the cheek and going inside.

Rhodes got in the car with Buddy, who radioed their destination to Hack. Hack said that he would telephone Mrs. Ramsey to let her know they were on their way.

When they got to within a half mile of Ramsey's house, Rhodes had Buddy cut the lights and slow down. They eased up to the yard at a crawl, as silently as it was possible for the car to travel. Buddy let the car drift to a stop without putting on the brakes.

The two men sat in the car looking around at the house and yard. There wasn't much of a moon in the sky, and the mercury vapor lamp in the yard wasn't burning. Either the electricity was off or the lamp had burned out. Or someone had deliberately put it out. There were no motorcycles to be seen, and there were no lights in the house.

"Reckon we ought to go in," Buddy said. "Otherwise we ain't never going to find out what's in there. If there's anything in there at all."

"I guess you're right," Rhodes said. "Front or back?"

"I always favored the back door, myself," Buddy said. "It's closer to the kitchen."

"That's as good a reason as any," Rhodes said. "Let's go."

They got out of the car, Buddy's gangling limbs making it a somewhat complicated exit. Running low, they reached the wall of the house, skirting the sides below the window level until they came to the back door. There was a screen door set in front of a wooden door. Both were closed, with no signs of a forced entry to be seen in the dim light.

"Who goes first?" Rhodes asked.

"You're the sheriff," Buddy said.

"So?"

"So you get to pick."

"I'll go first, then. You be ready." The screen door opened outward, and Rhodes pulled on it gently. It wasn't locked. He stood up, Buddy behind him, and tried the doorknob of the inner door. It turned easily.

"Reckon Miz Ramsey'd leave that door unlocked?" Buddy whispered.

Rhodes shook his head, no. He knew what was in that house, the ovens, the TV set, the VCR. It was all worth too much money to be left behind an unlocked door. Unless, of course, Mrs. Ramsey was very careless. He didn't think she was careless. He pulled out his pistol. Buddy followed suit. He gave the door a gentle push and watched it swing open.

There was no movement from inside the house. All the blinds had been drawn shut, and it was very dark. How had Mrs. Ramsey seen lights moving around? Something was wrong. Rhodes was just about to tell Buddy to radio Hack to send Ruth Grady out when he heard Rapper's voice behind them.

"I was beginning to think you wouldn't be showing up, Sheriff," Rapper said. "Don't bother to turn around. I'm holding a gun on you. Your own gun, as a matter of fact. Why don't you and your deputy just step on inside and we can get this over with." Rhodes started to move. "Lay the guns down first," Rapper said. "Right there on the ground will be fine. Do it!"

Whereas Rapper's voice had seemed calm at first, the last two words ripped through the night with vicious intent. Rhodes and Buddy lay down their pistols and stepped inside the house. Rapper followed closely behind them.

"Get the shades up," Rapper said. Rhodes heard rummaging around in the darkness, then the sounds of shades flapping up. There was a little more light in the room, though not much, and he could make out the forms of Nellie and Wyneva. There were two wooden chairs from Ramsey's table in the middle of the room.

"You two can just sit in those chairs," Rapper said.

Buddy and Rhodes did as they were told. While Rapper held the pistol on them, Nellie tied their hands and feet with nylon cord. Their arms were tied behind them, but they were not tied to the backs of the chairs.

"Now then, Sheriff," Rapper said after they were tied and Nellie had stepped away. "I want you to know that I'm going to enjoy this. You've caused me a lot of trouble, and we heard tonight that Jayse talked. So I guess you know what's growing down behind this house. Well, I won't be getting it now, but that's not what's bothering me. Not really. What's bothering me is the way you've been on my case. I don't like to have to run, not from you or anybody else. But you've caught me with my pants down twice. Now I've caught you. And you're going to hurt a lot more than I have."

"What about my deputy?" Rhodes asked. "He's never even seen you before."

"Tough luck," Rapper said, laughing a little. "He ought to keep better company."

Rhodes figured it was no use to make idle threats. Hack knew where they were, but it was doubtful that he would send anybody in time to help them. He would never guess that they were dumb enough to have fallen into a trap. And it wouldn't do any good to mention Cox and Malvin; it appeared likely that Rapper didn't know about them. But if he didn't, then why had Cullens been killed? Maybe he had died before he could tell anything, or maybe he had been well trained. Rhodes decided to ask. He didn't have anything to lose.

"Are you going to kill us like you did Buster Cullens?" he asked.

Rapper laughed again. It wasn't a pleasant sound in the dark house. "Cullens was sticking his nose in. He got what he deserved. I didn't do it, though. Me and the boys found him like that."

"Sure you did," Rhodes said. "That's why Jayse had that axe handle in his hands."

Rapper stepped up and slapped Rhodes across the face with the back of his hand, almost knocking Rhodes out of the chair. "It's time for the first lesson, Sheriff," Rapper said, as casually as if he were talking to a clerk in the supermarket. "You don't crack wise with me. Not when I feel about you the way I do. Now, let's start over. Me and the boys found Cullens like that."

Rhodes thought about it. There was something behind Rapper's words, but Rhodes couldn't quite figure out what it was. "You know who killed him, though."

"That's better," Rapper said. "That's a lot better. A little respect, Sheriff, that's all I want."

The man was definitely a major lunatic, Rhodes thought. Unfortunately, he was a major lunatic with the upper hand. "So I guess you're going to do my job for me and tell me who it was."

"I can do that, if I want to," Rapper said. "But it seems to me that Jayse would have told you already if he'd talked. I wonder about that. Could it be that you've been telling lies, Sheriff? I really hate that. I really do." He reached out and backhanded Rhodes again, even harder than the first time. Rhodes tasted blood in his mouth.

"You see," Rapper said calmly, "I don't like for people to lie to me. People are always lying to me and about me. I don't like that. Do I, Nellie?"

"No," Nellie said, sounding a little surprised at being addressed. "You don't like that, Rapper. I don't know why people are always doing that. It just gets them in trouble."

The funny part was, Rhodes thought, Rapper didn't look crazy. He looked like a short, pudgy little man, like he might be a schoolteacher or a salesman. The meanness was in his eyes, and Rhodes couldn't see them in the dark.

154

"Well, enough of this stalling around," Rapper said. "It's time to get down to business, so to speak. I think I'll let you hear about it from Wyneva. Tell them why you killed their friend Buster."

Wyneva stepped near Rhodes, but not too near. "He killed Bert," she said. "He never really loved me, and he had to get back at the only man who did."

Rhodes didn't know what was going through Buddy's mind during all of this, but his own thoughts were racing a mile a minute. He was trying to put all the facts together, just on the off chance he ever got to tell a jury about them.

"I don't understand it," Rhodes said, honestly enough. He wasn't stalling. He really couldn't figure it out.

"Tell him," Rapper said. "We have time."

"OK," Wyneva said. "I guess it won't hurt." She paused to organize her thoughts and then began. "I was living with Bert Ramsey for a while. That was Rapper's idea. He'd heard from somebody that Bert had been a member of Los Muertos, and he thought he could maybe con Bert into growing a little weed for us, Bert having a little piece of land and all. So he sent me to get to know him and see what was what. Me and Bert, we just sort of hit it off, you know? It wasn't like I was doing a job or anything. We really got along."

She stopped, maybe thinking about Bert. Rhodes thought he could see where the story was going now, but he wasn't going to rush it. He wasn't looking forward to whatever was coming up after it was all told. Nellie had tied them awfully tight, though, and Rhodes was beginning to lose the feeling in his hands. Maybe it would be better if they just went ahead and got it over with.

"Then I met Buster," Wyneva said. "He was cute, cuter than Bert, but Bert was already making money for us. I wasn't going to leave him. Besides, like I said, me and Bert really had something going for us.

"But Buster just wouldn't quit. He knew how to talk, and he knew how to treat a woman. He just kept on. So maybe I gave in a little. I don't know. That's when he started with the questions."

"Wyneva may look dumb, but she's not," Rapper said.

"Yeah," Wyneva said. "I'm not dumb. Guys think that, but I'm not. I knew right off where he was headed, but he fooled me a little bit. I wasn't sure if he was a single or if there was someone in it with him. I mean, I thought he might just be planning to rip Bert off or something, but there could've been more to it than that. Those damn narcs are all around these days."

Rhodes thought about Cox and Malvin again, and he wondered how much Rapper knew.

"We weren't worried about you local boys," Wyneva said. Rhodes was just as glad he couldn't see her face in the darkness. He could feel her contempt, and that was enough. He'd been fooled like a ten-year-old by Bert Ramsey and Rapper. They could have gone on growing dope in Blacklin County forever, and he'd never have known if Bert hadn't been killed.

"You fellas were fat and lazy," Wyneva said. "All Bert had to do was clear off a little land and go into business. Nobody would suspect him, and it was pretty easy to persuade him, really."

"Easy for Wyneva," Rapper said. "With a little persuasion from me and the boys. The money didn't hurt, either."

"We had it all going our way until that Buster Cullens showed up," Wyneva said. "So I went along with him to find out what he knew. He was close-mouthed, I'll give him that. There was no way I was going to find out anything from him."

"That day I saw you. . . ." Rhodes started.

"I thought you'd blown it all that day," Wyneva said. "And then when you said that Bert was dead, that did it. I really liked Bert."

"You didn't kill him, then?"

"Bert? Me?" Wyneva's voice rose sharply.

"Let's drop it," Rapper said. Bert's death was obviously a subject that he didn't want to discuss. "Finish up about Cullens," he said.

"I caught him off guard," Wyneva said. "I hit him with the axe handle, and then I tied him up. Just about like you two are tied now. And I just worked him over."

Her voice was cold and level, and it scared Rhodes more than Rapper's. Rapper was crazy, but Wyneva had an icy control that was truly frightening.

"He told me lots of things," Wyneva said.

Rhodes could imagine. He thought about an axe handle smacking into his ribs or the side of his head. It wasn't an experience he looked forward to.

"He said he loved me, but I knew that for a lie," Wyneva said. "That was at first. He got more truthful as things went on. He was a free-lancer, all right, heard a rumor and tried to cash in. Too bad for him."

"So you killed him," Rhodes said, thinking that Cox and Malvin would be proud of Cullens if anybody got to tell them about him. He really didn't expect that he'd be the one.

"I didn't really kill him," Wyneva said. "You might say he just killed himself. He could have told me what I needed to know anytime."

"Why kill him, then?" Rhodes asked. "Why not weeks ago? Or ever?"

"Because of Bert!" The rising voice again.

"But Cullens didn't have anything to do with Bert's death," Rhodes said. "That's not possible. He—"

"Shut up," Rapper said. "That's enough talking. I'm tired of you, Sheriff. Really tired. I looked around Ramsey's toolshed, but I couldn't find an axe handle. I think a hoe handle will do nicely, though. Get it, Nellie."

Nellie moved toward the door.

"Wait a minute," Rhodes said. "Wyneva . . ."

Rapper slapped him across the face again.

Rhodes wasn't quite sure exactly what happened next because his head wasn't clear. Buddy, however, had been waiting for his chance, and since Nellie was almost out of the room and Rapper and Wyneva had their attention focused on Rhodes, he took it.

Buddy lurched out of his sitting position, lowered his head, and butted Rapper.

Rhodes, leaning precariously in his chair, let himself fall the rest of the way. When he hit the floor he rolled toward Wyneva, knocking her off balance.

Wyneva fell, and Rhodes tried to get to his feet. He couldn't make it, so he kept on rolling, hoping that Buddy was all right, that Rapper had dropped the pistol, that Nellie hadn't gotten the handle yet.

There was a lot of thrashing around in the middle of the floor. Rapper was yelling, but Rhodes couldn't make out the words. He hit the wall, and using it to brace himself got to his feet.

He could see the outlines of bodies in the middle of the room, but he couldn't tell who was doing what to whom. The one he thought was Wyneva was bent over on hands and knees. The rest was a squirming mass made up of Buddy, Rapper, and Nellie. All of them were snorting and gasping. Buddy must have been holding his own, even with his hands and feet tied.

Rhodes didn't know what to do. He could hop into the kitchen and try to get untied, or he could throw himself into the middle of the melée. He didn't see much future in either course, but the latter idea seemed like something out of *Abbott and Costello Meet the Keystone Cops,* lacking only a few pies in the face. He started hopping toward the kitchen, keeping his shoulder near the wall.

It didn't take long. He backed up to the counter and, with his back to the drawers, pulled them all out, feeling for knives with his nearly numb fingers. He found them where he should have begun, in the drawer nearest the sink, and managed to get his hands on the handle of a reasonably-sized knife with a slick plastic handle.

Getting the knife blade in contact with the bonds that held his wrists was the next trick. First he dropped the knife.

Bracing himself against the counter, he slid down to the floor and fumbled around for the knife. This time he did better. Bracing against the counter seemed to help. Carefully, he eased the blade up between the rope. Then, as best he could he began sawing. He was pretty sure he was sawing on himself as much as the rope, but that couldn't be helped.

The noises from the next room were becoming more easy to distinguish from one another, and as he sawed he listened. He was pretty sure Buddy was getting the worst of things. It became pretty obvious when he heard Rapper say clearly, "Hit the sonofabitch with the chair."

There was a sickening thud. Ramsey's chairs weren't movie chairs that splintered on contact. They were real, solid, hardwood chairs that were built to take all sorts of punishment.

"Where's that goddamn Sheriff?" Rapper yelled.

Rhodes felt the rope part, and he snapped his wrists apart. He bent to cut the rope at his feet.

Then he heard three thunderously loud gunshots.

18

HAD IT BEEN physically possible, Rhodes would have jumped several feet in the air. It just wasn't possible. He did hit the floor flat on his belly, throwing the knife away across the room in the process.

The previous confusion in the other room was nothing to what it was now. There was another shot, and a huge hole was punched through the Sheetrock of the kitchen wall. There was a smashing and tinkling of glass. There were yells, and Wyneva screamed.

Over it all was the sound of Mrs. Ramsey's voice. "I'll get all you murderin' scum!" she yelled. There was a fifth shot.

Rhodes staggered up. "Mrs. Ramsey! This is Sheriff Dan Rhodes! Stop the shooting!"

"Don't you worry, Sheriff! I got 'em covered. All 'cept that one that went out the window!"

"Get some lights on," Rhodes called. "My deputy's in there. Get him untied. I'm going after the one outside." He had to trust Mrs. Ramsey to keep things under control. He was pretty sure that Rapper would be the one who got away. He went out the kitchen door, stumbling along, feeling the needles in his hands and feet as the circulation began to return.

He was unarmed, and he hoped Rapper was, but if Rapper got to his bike he would be hard to stop.

As if to taunt Rhodes, the sound of Rapper's bike came from Ramsey's shed. Rhodes could see the beam from the headlight. He began looking for something to stop Rapper.

There wasn't anything, and then Rapper came roaring out of the shed and right straight at Rhodes, pinned there in the headlight beam. Rhodes shifted to the left, and the beam followed him. Rapper intended to run him down.

Rhodes stood his ground, staring right into the headlight, trying to guess if Rapper would really do it. He thought the answer was that Rapper certainly would. At the last minute, just as the bike was about to smash him, Rhodes feinted left and dived to the right.

Rapper went with the feint and went by Rhodes's diving figure in a rush of sound. Rhodes clambered to his feet to see Rapper doing a sliding 180-degree turn, and then the headlight was coming back again.

Rhodes started forward to meet it, then tripped. He had found the hoe handle that Nellie had been going after earlier. He grabbed the handle and rolled to the left, just in time to avoid being bashed in the head by Rapper's front tire. Small clods of dirt thrown by the tire stung his cheeks.

Rhodes pushed himself erect with the help of the handle. He'd been taking such a beating lately that his whole body was beginning to feel like one giant bruise.

Rapper spun the bike again, pointing the light at Rhodes.

Rhodes held the handle behind him, waiting for Rapper's charge. He felt a little like Errol Flynn waiting for the Sioux in *They Died with Their Boots On*. His rifle was out of bullets, but he could use it as a club. . . .

It would have been a good idea if it had worked, but Rapper didn't go with the feint. Rhodes leaned right, but the headlight never wavered. It was too late to jump back to the left, so Rhodes tried to let his body go all the way right. Rapper wasn't fooled.

He didn't quite hit Rhodes head-on, however. The

last-minute lean had carried Rhodes just beyond the bike, and Rapper, having been fooled once, didn't want to swerve too far.

For the smallest fraction of a second, Rhodes thought he'd made it, but Rapper stuck out his leg just a little and caught him on the thigh.

If Rapper had been going fast, Rhodes would have been hurt badly. As it was, he felt the solid thunk of Rapper's booted foot and the equally solid whump of his back meeting the ground. Rapper was coming back at him by the time he got up.

Rhodes ran at him, giving it all he had, the hoe handle straight out in front of him like a lance. Rapper saw it and turned the bike aside. Rhodes swung the handle.

It caught Rapper in the upper arms and on the shoulders, and the effect was almost magical. It was as if Rapper had been lifted off the motorcycle by a giant hand reaching down to pluck him from the seat. The bike continued on across the yard without him, as Rapper landed hard on his back.

The handle was jerked from Rhodes's grip by the impact, and he jumped on Rapper, trying to subdue him. Most of Rapper's breath was gone, but he fought back by instinct.

Behind them, the motorcycle hit the side of the shed with a loud cracking of weathered boards and fell on its side, the motor still roaring.

Rhodes, not feeling much stronger than Rapper, got off a few weak punches, which had no effect on Rapper at all. Rapper, sucking great gulps of air, shoved Rhodes aside.

Both men got unsteadily to their feet. Rapper put his head down and made a lumbering charge at the sheriff. Rhodes managed to step aside and hit him in the back of the neck with clenched fists, but Rapper didn't go down. He turned and threw a wild punch that caught Rhodes a glancing blow on the right cheek and opened up the cut in Rhodes's mouth.

Rapper looped another punch, which Rhodes blocked with his left. Rhodes then sank a hard right in Rapper's pudgy stomach. Bad air whoofed out of Rapper's mouth, and he staggered backward toward the fallen motorcycle. Rhodes followed and hit him again.

It wasn't much of a blow, but Rapper stumbled on a rock and tumbled back, flailing his arms, trying to regain his balance. He couldn't quite do it.

Probably the motorcycle should have shut itself off when it fell over, Rhodes thought later, but it didn't. The chain was still engaged, and the back wheel was still spinning. Rapper's left hand dropped in among the spokes.

Rapper screamed.

If he'd been thinking, Rhodes might have tried to find the ends of Rapper's fingers. Maybe the doctor could have done something with them. By the time he *did* think about it, the next day, it was too late. He didn't even bother to go and look for them. He'd had too many loose body parts to take care of lately.

The engine of the motorcycle sputtered and died.

"Need any help, Sheriff?" Buddy called from the back door.

Rhodes felt a little like someone who'd been run over by a herd of rogue elephants. There was probably somewhere that he didn't ache, but he couldn't identify the spot.

Buddy and Mrs. Ramsey had tied Wyneva and Nellie, and then Buddy had yelled for Rhodes. He'd come out and helped Rhodes drag Rapper into the house, where they'd stopped the bleeding and tied him as well.

Mrs. Ramsey was telling her story. "So when the lights never came back on, I figured you all hadn't come to see about things. I went to the gun cabinet and got my husband's old thirty ought-six and came to see if I could find out what was goin' on. A lucky thing, too."

Rhodes didn't feel like the time was right for a speech on the dangers of citizens taking the law into their own hands. "Yes, it was," he said. Buddy was at the car, radioing Hack.

"That woman has caused me grief," Mrs. Ramsey said. "It's the dope that's ruinin' the nation. People like her have got to be stopped."

Mrs. Ramsey sat stolidly in one of the wooden chairs where Rhodes and Buddy had been tied. Rhodes sat in the other, his head drooping down on his chest. He was almost too tired to answer. "You're right," he said.

Wyneva, Nellie, and Rapper, tied hand and foot, were propped against the wall of the room. Mrs. Ramsey's rifle was safely out of their reach, and safely out of Mrs. Ramsey's reach for that matter. Rapper was in even worse shape than Rhodes, barely conscious. Nellie and Wyneva sat quietly, seemingly with little to say.

Mrs. Ramsey was the only one who felt like talking. "She took Bert, and she turned him," she said, looking malevolently at Wyneva. "He was a fine man, until she turned him. She's to blame."

"That's not so," Wyneva said. Rhodes looked up. "Bert and me got along," Wyneva said. "I really liked Bert. More than anybody, ever."

"Humph," Mrs. Ramsey said.

It was very late when Rhodes got home, but he remembered to feed the dog, who was waiting patiently in the backyard. He also refilled the water dish. Then he went inside.

The late movie was *The Magnificent Seven*. Rhodes tried to stay awake for his favorite line, when Horst Buckholtz tells Yul Brynner that the men of the Mexican village have hidden their women for fear that Brynner and his gunslingers might rape them. "Well," says Brynner, "we might."

He didn't make it, though. He went to sleep while Brynner and Steve McQueen were still driving the hearse to Boot Hill.

Rhodes was at the jail early the next morning. Rapper, Nellie, and Wyneva had been booked in the previous night. Malvin and Cox were due to arrive at nine-thirty for their chance at questioning them, and Rhodes, who had been simply too tired the night before, wanted to get a few minutes with them first.

Before he could get to them, however, he had to get through Hack. "Mornin', Sheriff," Hack said.

Rhodes waited. He knew something more was coming. It usually did.

"You feelin' better today?" Hack was being solicitous, something he liked to practice on occasion, to put off telling what was really on his mind.

"I'm fine, Hack," Rhodes said. "I guess we made things a little hectic in here last night. I was pretty tired after it was all over. How about yourself?"

It was the opening Hack had been waiting for. "I was pretty tired, too," he said. "But I didn't get to go right to sleep like some people. I tried to sack out on my cot, but you might know there'd be trouble."

Now he was getting to the heart of the matter. "What kind of trouble?" Rhodes asked.

"Damned rabbit hunter," Hack said.

"Rabbit hunter?" Rhodes asked. "It must have been two o'clock in the morning."

" 'Bout that," Hack said. "That was the trouble."

Hack stopped. Rhodes knew that Hack wanted him to say something to urge him on, but Rhodes couldn't think of anything. So he just sat and waited.

"Well," Hack said finally, "there was this fella who

waved Ruth Grady down. Wanted to buy a permit to shoot rabbits at night, he said. Said he used to do that all the time up in Arkansas when he was a boy and wanted to give it a try here. Spotlight 'em, he said. Like deer.''

"That's illegal," Rhodes said. "Deer and rabbits both. Maybe they don't know that in Arkansas.''

"They don't know diddly in Arkansas, if you ask me," Hack said. "Anyway, Ruth told him about it bein' illegal. Then he wanted to know if she was a real deputy sheriff. Them people in Arkansas got a hell of a nerve. She could tell he was about three sheets to the wind, so she brought him in. He's still sleepin' it off upstairs.''

Rhodes had to restrain his laughter. Hack's indignation was comical enough on its own, but based on Hack's past feelings about Ruth Grady it was downright hilarious. Rhodes kept a straight face with difficulty. "I hope the judge sets a high bail," he said.

"Damn right," Hack said. "Damn Arkansas.''

Rhodes went back to the cell area. The cells were old and uncomfortable. The mattresses were thin, the pipes were rusty. Blacklin County needed a new jail, and before too long they would have to build one. Or else some judge would order them to do it. So far no prisoners had complained, but that was probably because Lawton took such good care of things. Everything was old, but everything was clean. Lawton was mopping the hall when Rhodes stopped in front of Rapper's cell.

"Did you give them a good breakfast today?" Hack asked.

"The best," Lawton said. "Miz Stutts outdid herself.''

Mrs. Stutts cooked for the jail. It was sort of a hobby for her, and she did it mostly as a favor to the county, which paid for the groceries and a little for her time. Mrs. Stutts's meals were another reason that no one had ever complained very strongly about the jail. Most prisoners would readily admit that they ate better there than anywhere else. Some got themselves arrested regularly around Thanksgiving, just for her dressing.

Rapper didn't look especially thrilled with what he had eaten, but his plate was clean. He sat on his cot, looking like a pudgy man with a problem, his oiled hair in disarray. He was leaning forward, with his elbows resting on his knees, his hands hanging down. The left hand was tied with a white bandage that was already beginning to look a bit dirty. He looked up as Rhodes stopped outside his cell.

The disappointing thing to Rhodes was that Rapper looked better than Rhodes did. Rhodes was sore in places that he didn't know could even get sore, but Rapper looked basically unscratched except for a few streaks of red on his face where the ground had scraped it. And, of course, his hand. Rhodes knew that under the bandage three of the fingers were shorter than they had been the night before.

Rapper looked up at Rhodes with bored eyes.

"I think we can tie you in to the Cullens murder as an accessory," Rhodes said by way of opening the conversation.

Rapper almost laughed. "If that's what you booked me for, I'll be out of here before you can read me my rights. I've already called my lawyer."

"There are a few other things," Rhodes said. "Like assault on a police officer, possession of a deadly weapon, conspiracy, intent to commit murder . . ."

Rapper stood up and walked over to the bars. "Don't try to shit me," he said. "I doubt any of that will stand up. Most of it's your word against mine. Yours and your deputy's maybe. Nothing solid. Nothing."

"Maybe," Rhodes said. "Maybe not. Then there's the dope. Lots of solid evidence there."

"Growing on Bert Ramsey's land," Rapper said, gripping the bars and smiling. Prove I ever had a connection with Ramsey. What Wyneva said last night? Forget it. She'll never say it again."

"Let's say we just forget it," Rhodes said. "Fine by me. Then we have you, Nellie, Jayse, all standing around in the room with a dead body and Jayse holding the murder weapon. You got a pretty good lawyer?"

"The best," Rapper said, the grin still in place. "Good enough to get Wyneva to admit the murder again if I want her to."

Rhodes hated Rapper for being able to stand up so easily. If Rhodes had been able to sit on a soft cot, he would have done so. He *had* to stand. He wished he'd been able to hurt Rapper more. Then he was sorry he'd wished it.

"All right," Rhodes said, "but there's still Bert Ramsey. We'll get you on that one. All I have to do is find the gun. And when I tell Wyneva that you killed Bert, she'll tell us everything she knows. The only riding you'll be doing then is in the prison rodeo down in Huntsville. No more motorcycles for you."

Rapper laughed, let go of the bars, and went back to sit on the cot, giving Rhodes a little satisfaction, but not much. Rhodes didn't like the laugh. It was entirely too confident.

"There's only one little problem with that idea, Sheriff," Rapper said.

"What's that?"

"You'll never find the gun." Rapper put his arms behind his head, lifted his feet up on the cot, and lay back.

"I'll find it," Rhodes said.

"It won't be easy," Rapper said to the ceiling.

"I didn't say it would be easy," Rhodes said. "I said I'd find it."

"How'll you prove it's mine?" Rapper asked, still looking up.

168

Rhodes paused. He didn't know.

"Anybody ever see me with a gun?" Rapper said, pressing it. "Did you? Except for your own pistol, of course."

"Fingerprints," Rhodes said, but he wasn't confident.

"What if I wiped it clean?" Rapper said. "Or better yet, what if I didn't kill Ramsey?"

Now it was Rhodes who was gripping the bars, looking in at Rapper. "If you didn't, who did?"

"How do I know? I'm not the sheriff." Rapper sat up. "Look, you've caught me and roughed me up, and I'm not complaining. I may even be guilty of a couple of things. Or maybe I'm not. But I'm not going to be set up for some stupid charge like murder. Think about it. Why would I kill Ramsey? The guy was a gold mine for me. We were raking it in. That is, we were if what you think is true. So why do I kill him? Answer that one." Rapper put his hands behind his head and lay back down.

Rhodes stood looking at him through the bars for a minute, then went out into the office. He sat in his chair that no longer squeaked and waited for Cox and Malvin.

19

Cox and Malvin had even less luck than Rhodes. Rapper refused to talk to them.

"There's no way we can really tie him to the stuff," Cox said. Malvin nodded in agreement. "We all know what he was doing in the county," Cox went on. "The Greer woman had to get in touch with him and let him know that she was suspicious of Cullens. Otherwise, I don't think he would have come around until time for a harvest. Apparently, though, Rapper is willing to let her take the fall for Cullens and trust that she won't implicate him. He may just walk out of this."

"He might," Rhodes said. "It's pretty obvious that we can get him on some assault charge, along with the others, but that might be the extent of things."

"They have a pretty clever operation going," Malvin said. "They find these little counties and they grow just a little patch of dope, not enough to call attention to themselves. Then they cut it and sell it somewhere else, never where they grow it. Rapper is just part of the whole operation, not the brains."

"He's pretty smart," Rhodes said.

"True enough," Cox said. "Smarter that we are, maybe."

At that minute, the jail door opened and a man walked in. He was dressed in a conservative blue suit with faint chalk-colored stripes in it, a suit that made the suits worn by Cox and Malvin look like something they'd picked up at a local discount store. He wore lots of gold—rings on both hands, and a thick gold watch. He was young, maybe thirty-two, with a smooth, unlined face. His hair had been carefully styled, and though it was not long, it was cut full and carefully layered. "I'm Wayne Gault," he said. "I believe you have my clients, Mr. Rapper and Mr. Nelson, in custody here." His rich baritone was carefully modulated, but Rhodes could tell that he could make it boom if he wanted to.

"Show him," Rhodes said to Lawton, who was sitting by Hack at the radio table.

Lawton got up and led Wayne Gault to the cells.

Cox and Malvin looked depressed. "At least we cut off the supply," Malvin said. "A lawyer like that, we don't have much chance of anything else. Looks like Los Muertos can afford the best."

"We'll get some indictments when all this comes to the grand jury," Rhodes said.

"Sure," Cox said. "But what do you think will happen when—or if—you get to court? How much can we really prove?"

"We can get them on the assault," Rhodes said. He knew it wasn't much. It certainly wasn't enough.

"And the Greer woman," Malvin said. "Don't forget her."

"I'm glad to get her," Cox said. "Damn her. If Buster had just gotten a little more information."

"Let's not speak ill of the dead," Malvin said.

"Damn," Cox said.

Rapper and Nellie were out on bail by early afternoon. Wyneva was clearly to be the scapegoat. She didn't even seem to mind it very much. Jayse and his buddy in the hospital would be free as soon as the doctor released them. Rhodes doubted that he would ever see any of the four again. They had made their bail and they would gladly forfeit it, just as long as they never had to come back to Blacklin County again. He had told Malvin and Cox that the assault charges would stick, but they would stick only if they could get the men in court. Rhodes figured that they would disappear in Houston or Dallas, or maybe even out of the state. It was a depressing thought.

It was equally depressing that Rapper had proved smarter than Rhodes thought he was. He had easily pointed out the flaws in Rhodes's own thinking. Rhodes wondered why he had even considered Rapper guilty of shooting Bert Ramsey in the first place.

Sitting at home in his chair, Rhodes was going over the whole thing one more time. He had left the jail after Rapper's lawyer had posted the bail. He had called Cox and Malvin first, then gotten into his pickup and left. He'd fed Speedo and eaten a sandwich, thinking he would watch the movie and think. The movie was *Hell's Angels on Wheels*. Rhodes turned it off.

He thought about all the things that had bothered him from the beginning. The first thing was Bert Ramsey's finding the boxes of amputated limbs. That was just coincidence. Had to be, and Rhodes was glad that at least that part of things had been brought to a more or less satisfactory ending. The contents of the boxes had been safely buried and could do no harm now, if they ever could have.

Anyone with normal curiosity would have opened those boxes, and Bert Ramsey was normal. When he saw what they contained, he decided to report them rather than take a chance on stirring up even bigger trouble. After all, they weren't found on his land, and there would be no call for Rhodes to do any searching there. Bert was clean on that one, and he'd probably figured that he could only get into more trouble by failing to report what he'd found if it turned out later than an axe-murderer was on the loose.

So did Dr. Rawlings kill Bert to retaliate for his finding what Dr. Rawlings was trying to dispose of quietly? That was too ridiculous for real consideration.

Were the murders of Cullens and Ramsey even connected? They had to be, somehow, Rhodes thought. But maybe not in the way he'd first imagined.

Rhodes prided himself on his ability to read people, to keep asking questions until he discovered the motives that led to crimes. He didn't have all the latest equipment, but he was persistent. This time, he'd been on the wrong track. Rapper had been there, and Rapper was convenient; so Rhodes had elected him as the most likely suspect. There was nothing particularly wrong with that, except that Rapper hadn't done it, and Rhodes had been led astray by concentrating on him.

Annoyed with himself, Rhodes clicked the movie back on, but at the first sight of a motorcycle he switched it off again.

Then a new thought occurred to him, one that he would never have considered earlier. There was something in the story that Wyneva had told, though. Suppose that Buster Cullens had tried to question Ramsey. Cullens was certainly overeager—even Wyneva had spotted his questions as being too obvious. Maybe he had seen that she was catching on and had decided to try his luck with Ramsey. Then the two had gotten into an argument, and Cullens had shot Ramsey.

That wouldn't wash, though. Where was the gun? That's what I should have been thinking more about all along, Rhodes realized. The gun. There was no gun in the run-down house where Cullens had lived, and there was no gun in Ramsey's house, either. Whoever had done the shooting had taken the gun with him. No gun had ever turned up anywhere around Rapper and his crew, but they could have gotten rid of it easily enough. Still. . . .

Rhodes got up and walked outside to the backyard. Speedo, in the shade of the tree, lifted his head and looked up. Rhodes sat on the back step, and the dog trotted over and sat down. Rhodes reached out and scratched its head. "Looks like you're getting pretty used to things around here," Rhodes said. Speedo thwacked his tail on the grass.

"It's all got to do with motorcycles and dope, some way or another," Rhodes said. Speedo lay down. Dope and motorcycles didn't interest him.

"That's right," Rhodes said. "Take it easy. Leave all the thinking to me." There were times when he wished he could live a dog's life, all right, and this was another one of them, but he couldn't. So he sat there on the steps and ran everything back through his mind, just as if he were watching a familiar movie.

And eventually he came up with the answer.

It wasn't the answer he wanted, but that didn't matter. It was the answer that fit, the only answer that really could have fit. Well, no one had ever said that life had to be perfect.

Rhodes stood up. A lot of time had passed as he sat on the step, and he was stiff. His rear end hurt, and his back was tired. He stretched upward, lifting his arms. Speedo watched but didn't move. He wasn't a dog given to overexertion.

"You never know, do you?" he said to Speedo.

Speedo didn't say a word.

Rhodes went inside and called Ivy.

"I really don't like it," Ivy said as they sat in her living room. "I know you have a dangerous job, but getting tied up in chairs, getting run over by motorcycles, getting into fistfights . . . it's just too much."

Rhodes could tell that she was really annoyed. He'd debated with himself about whether to tell her about last night's events, but he'd decided that honesty was really the best policy in this case. After all, they were going to be married. She had to know what she was getting into. "Well," he said, "I wasn't actually run over by the motorcycle."

Ivy looked at him. "It doesn't make any difference.

It's the same thing. You're lucky you're not in the hospital again."

She was referring to another recent case, after which Rhodes had wound up in even worse condition than he was in now. It wasn't a case that he particularly liked to remember. "But I'm *not* in the hospital," he said.

"And whose fault is that? You've been hit with axe handles, too, and it's a wonder that Rapper didn't shoot you. I just don't know how you can keep on dealing with that kind of person."

"It's part of the job," Rhodes said. "That's what I wanted to tell you. But that's not all of it."

"There's more?"

"There's worse," he said, and then he told her.

"Well," she said when he was finished.

"I told you," he said.

"You were right," she said. "It's worse. Are you sure, though?"

"I'm sure. I can't prove it, but I'm sure."

"If you can't prove it, what are you going to do?"

"Get a confession, I expect," Rhodes said.

"Just like that?" Ivy asked.

"Probably not," Rhodes said. "But I think it'll come pretty easy. I thought you might like to be there."

"Me?"

"You felt sorry for her before," he said.

"And I still do. Even more now, if you're right. Are you *sure* you're right?"

"As sure as I ever am about anything," he said.

"All right," Ivy said. "I'll go."

Rhodes had one of the county cars back now, and they drove out to Eller's Prairie in it. He parked in front of Mrs. Ramsey's house, just as the sun was going down. They got out and Rhodes knocked. Mrs. Ramsey's voice called for them to come in.

Mrs. Ramsey was sitting in her living room with the TV set on. She had the sound turned very low, and she didn't seem to be watching it. It was just on to keep her company. "Hello, Sheriff," she said as they walked in. "Mrs. Daniel."

"Good evening, Mrs. Ramsey," Rhodes said. Ivy didn't speak. Rhodes had told her on the drive out that she didn't need to play a part in the proceedings. He just wanted her there for moral support. He wasn't looking forward to what he had to do, but it was his job. Her being there would make it a little easier for him, he thought, and maybe for Mrs. Ramsey.

Mrs. Ramsey sat in her chair, not making any move to get up. She looked dull and listless. "What can I do for you?" she asked.

"I think you know that," Rhodes said. "Do you mind if we sit down?"

Mrs. Ramsey made an idle gesture with her thick wrist as if to indicate the other chairs, but she didn't say anything. Rhodes sat where he could look into her face, and Ivy sat nearby.

"I need to talk to you about Bert," Rhodes said.

Mrs. Ramsey shook her head but still said nothing.

"You knew about what he was doing, didn't you?" Rhodes asked.

Mrs. Ramsey nodded. Rhodes waited. "It was that woman that ruined him," Mrs. Ramsey finally said.

"He was a good man," Ivy said. "He put in some flower beds for me once. He really had a skill for working like that."

Mrs. Ramsey didn't look at her. She seemed to be staring inward more than looking at anything in the room around her. "He surely did," she said. "He was a fine boy. It was that woman."

"She's the one, all right," Rhodes said. "If it hadn't been for her, he'd never have gotten into growing that dope. I know that. How did you find it out?"

"It was the money," Mrs. Ramsey said. "All that money. He bought things for me. I knew he wasn't earnin' that kind of money from puttin' in flower beds. It had to be somethin' else. He finally told me what it was."

Now that she had started, Mrs. Ramsey didn't need much coaching. "You knew Los Muertos was mixed up in it," Rhodes said.

"Those motorsickles," Mrs. Ramsey said. "He got away from that a long time ago, and that woman brought it all back."

"The night Bert was mu—the night he died, you didn't really hear anything, did you?" Rhodes asked.

"Naw, I never did. That Buster Cullens, he was one of 'em, though, and he had a motorsickle. They were around, somewhere. It was all their fault, them and that woman. They ought to all be in the pen."

Rhodes agreed, and he hated to tell her that they weren't in jail, except for Wyneva, and that they weren't likely to be. The one in jail would be Mrs. Ramsey. It was pretty much as he'd thought, so far. All the little things that Mrs. Ramsey had said pointed that way. It was Wyneva and Rapper and the rest that she wanted to punish. They were really to blame for Bert's death, she thought, and Rhodes had to admit that she had a point. They hadn't pulled the trigger, though.

"Do you have a shotgun, Mrs. Ramsey?" he asked.

"My husband's old Remington automatic is in the gun cabinet," she said.

"I expect you carried it with you when you went down to talk to Bert last Saturday night, didn't you? In case you met any of his friends along the way?"

"I guess I did," Mrs. Ramsey said. "I guess that's right."

"What happened then?" Rhodes asked, though he thought he knew. Mrs. Ramsey had expressed her feelings about dope pretty clearly, already.

Mrs. Ramsey sighed. "I told Bert that he'd have to

give up doin' what he was doin'. I told him that it was the Devil's work that he was into, and that he'd lost the woman, and that it was time to stop."

"And he didn't want to?"

"It was the money," Mrs. Ramsey said. "He got to where he liked it. You don't know how it is, to have all that money. He had plenty for what he needed, just by doing jobs around town, but after he was getting so much, he got to where he liked it."

The large old woman shook her head and closed her eyes. Her chin sank slowly toward her chest. "I didn't go to kill him," she said. "But that dope is the ruination of the world."

Those words, or something like them, were what had not quite registered on Rhodes the previous night. If he hadn't been so tired, so beaten up, maybe he would have caught on sooner. No one had told Mrs. Ramsey that Bert had been involved with marijuana. Cox and Malvin hadn't talked to her, and Rhodes certainly hadn't told her. But she had known, and with her attitude being what it was, she couldn't have been happy. So she'd talked to Bert about it.

"He argued with me," she said. "Told me that if he didn't do it, someone else would. I guess we got to yellin'. I . . . I didn't point the gun at him, but it got in his face. He grabbed the barrel, and then it just . . . it just. . . ."

Ivy reached out and put her hand on Mrs. Ramsey's hand. "It's all right," she said. "We know you didn't mean to do it."

Large tears rolled down Mrs. Ramsey's cheeks. "No," she said, "I didn't mean to do it."

20

LATER THAT NIGHT, after they had carried Mrs. Ramsey to the jail and gotten Lawton to install her in the "good" cell, Ivy asked Rhodes, "What do you think really happened?"

They were sitting outside her house in the county car. Rhodes wasn't feeling particularly romantic, and he sensed that Ivy wasn't either. "I think she's telling the truth, as she sees it," he said. "I don't know that we'll ever find out exactly what happened."

Ivy curled one leg up under her and turned to face him in the front seat. "What does that mean?"

"I'm not trying to hide anything," Rhodes said. "It's just that what she believes happened and what really happened may not be the same thing. I mean, she really thinks that it wasn't her fault. It was Rapper's fault. Or it was Wyneva's fault. Failing all that, it was Bert's fault. But it wasn't her fault."

"You mean that she can't admit it to herself, even if it's true that she went there with the intention of shooting him," Ivy said.

"Maybe that's what I mean," Rhodes said. "I'm just a sheriff, not a psychologist. They have those in cities, but we don't have one here."

"You seem to do all right," Ivy said.

"Yeah, but it's no fun," Rhodes said. "I'll always wonder about a few things."

"Such as?"

"Such as why she gave me the story about the motor-cycles. Had she really heard them? Why try to put the blame on Buster Cullens? He was a likely suspect, in a way, but would she have let him be arrested? And why wait until the next morning to report the murder? That's the thing that the prosecutor will hammer into the jury, if she's tried for murder."

" 'If'?"

"If. Somehow I doubt that anyone will want that. I imagine that she'll go to trial on a reduced charge and get a light sentence. Probably probated."

"And do you care?"

Rhodes wasn't sure how to answer that. If he had known for sure what had happened that Saturday night when Mrs. Ramsey picked up the shotgun and walked out of her house, he could have answered with certainty. But he didn't know, and he never would. "I care more about Rapper," he said finally.

"I'm glad you care," Ivy said. Then, after a minute, "At least one good thing came out of all this."

"What?"

"You got yourself a dog."

It got hot early the next morning. Rhodes went out to the backyard to check on the dog, who was already asleep under the shade tree. Rhodes put out some fresh food and water, but Speedo took very little interest. He had settled in, now, and he knew there would be food and water whenever he wanted it. Rhodes walked over and scratched the dog's head, then drove to the jail.

Hack and Lawton were waiting expectantly when he walked in. That meant that there was something going on, but he was determined to go on the attack first. "How's Mrs. Ramsey doing?" he asked.

"Fine, just fine," Lawton said. " 'Course, that cot's not near close to bein' big enough for her, but she did all right. I think she spent most of the night readin' one of those Gideon Bibles. Anyway, Ruth's back there with her right now, seein' that she's comfortable. I put that Wyneva up on the second floor."

"Judge ought to be settin' bail for Miz Ramsey before too long," Hack said. "I don't expect she'll be around by this afternoon."

"She called a lawyer yet?" Rhodes asked. He wanted to be sure a lawyer was present when Mrs. Ramsey was informed of all her rights and while she gave her legal confession.

"Not yet," Hack said. "You goin' to ask the judge to appoint one?"

"I think I'll get her to call Painter," Rhodes said. "He's a good one, and he'll take the case, I think."

"Good idea," Hack said. The expectant look was back on his face.

OK, Rhodes thought, I might as well dive in. "Any calls this morning?" he asked.

It was what they had been waiting for. "Two," Lawton said happily. Hack was quiet, letting Lawton have the only line he was likely to get in the conversation.

"Ah," Rhodes said, dragging it out to see if he could avoid having to ask who had called.

"One of 'em was from Clyde Ballinger," Lawton said.

Hack clamped his teeth together, but he managed not to say anything. He was giving Lawton a lot of rope today.

"Clyde Ballinger?" Rhodes was actually surprised, and the question popped out before he thought. "What did he want?"

"Seems like after you and Ivy left the buryin' the other afternoon, one of his helpers slipped and turned his ankle while he was fillin' in the grave," Hack said. "He wants to know if the county is insured for that sort of thing."

Rhodes had been holding his breath. Now he let it out

in a lengthy sigh. "I was afraid he'd found out something about those arms and legs that would change things around," he said. "You can tell him that the county isn't liable if he calls again, but don't bother to call him. That little job was purely private enterprise, even if he was doing me a favor."

"That's what I thought," Hack said. "I'll tell him. He said it reminded him of somethin' out of a book, but I can't recall what he said the name of it was."

"Never mind," Rhodes said. He looked at Hack. He knew they were saving the second call for the last because it was the best. It was always like that.

This time they out-waited him. "All right," he said after a minute or two, "who was the other call from?"

"The preacher," Lawton said.

There were more churches in Blacklin County than there were people, someone had once said. That made for a lot of preachers, too. "Which one?" Rhodes asked.

"Where the demonstration was," Hack said.

"The Reverend Funk," Rhodes said. "And there wasn't a demonstration."

"That's the one," Hack said.

"Fine," Rhodes said. "What did the reverend want today? I hope there hasn't been another disturbance."

"Not exactly," said Ruth Grady as she stepped through the door leading to the cell block. "But it's pretty close."

"Good morning, Ruth," Rhodes said. "I hope you aren't getting like these two old reprobates."

Ruth Grady smiled. "Well, they've been letting me hang around a little. Hack's been teaching me about the radio."

"She's pickin' it up pretty dern quick, too," Hack said. "Before long, she'll know near about as much as I do."

"Now, Hack, you know better than that," Ruth said.

She winked at Rhodes over Hack's head. Rhodes had to smile.

"Don't you laugh, Sheriff," Hack said. "I know you don't think much of how smart some women can be, but some of us are more . . . uh, liberated, than you are."

"I guess that's right," Rhodes said. "But I'm trying to improve myself. Now, back to Reverend Funk."

"Oh, yeah," Hack said. "Seems he had a crowd on the church parkin' lot last night and this mornin'. He called to complain about it and asked for a little help. I told him that the sheriff'd have to deal with it."

"First time I ever heard a preacher complain about a crowd," Rhodes said. "But you say this one stayed all night?"

"All night," Hack said. "Messed up that parkin' lot somethin' awful."

"Messed it up how?"

Hack looked at Ruth Grady, who was standing with a very straight face. "Well, they *messed* it up," he said.

Rhodes didn't get it. He looked at Ruth, too.

To keep from laughing, Ruth said, "It was cows, Sheriff. The crowd was a herd of cows. They spent the night on the church parking lot."

"Oh," Rhodes said.

"That preacher's hoppin' mad," Lawton said.

"Mad ain't the word," Hack said. "They call it 'wrath' in the Bible."

"Same thing," Lawton said.

"Anyway," Hack said, "he says it's Mr. Clawson's cows. You know, he has that little feedlot three or four blocks from the church. I guess the fence broke. Reverend Funk's been out on that parkin' lot most of the mornin', so far, with a shovel and some plastic garbage bags. He wants you to arrest Mr. Clawson and put him on the other end of a shovel. If you won't do that, he wants you down there yourself."

"He's kidding," Rhodes said.

"I don't think so," Ruth said.

"You're the sheriff," Hack said.

"Seems like I've heard that one before," Rhodes said.

That evening Rhodes and Ivy were eating supper at the Bluebonnet—hamburgers and Dr Peppers, Rhodes's favorite. Ivy wanted to know how his day had been.

"You probably wouldn't believe me if I told you," Rhodes said.

"Considering the things I've seen, heard, and done in the last few days just being around you, I'd believe just about anything," Ivy said.

"Speaking of that, you never did tell me about learning to ride a motorcycle," Rhodes said. He thought fleetingly of Ivy's legs and how they had looked when she hiked up her skirt. He looked down at his Dr Pepper in case he was blushing.

"I told you, my brother taught me," Ivy said. "He had a bike when we were teenagers, and I wanted to learn to ride. We had to go out to an old field on the far side of town so my mother wouldn't catch us. She'd have died if she had known."

Rhodes looked wistful. "I always sort of wanted to own a motorcycle," he said.

"It's fun, but it's dangerous," Ivy said. "And look at the kind of people it can get you involved with."

"That's the truth," Rhodes said.

"Now, about your day," Ivy said.

Rhodes told her.

Ivy laughed. "Do you get any extra pay for that?" she asked.

Rhodes shook his head. "I even had to provide my own shovel," he said.

"Maybe your job isn't as glamorous and exciting as I thought," Ivy said.

184

"Oh, I don't know," Rhodes said. "Tomorrow, two government guys are going to show me how to burn a whole field of marijuana."

"Now that *does* sound exciting," Ivy said.

Rhodes shook his head again. "No," he said biting into the last chunk of his hamburger. "It's the same thing. We just won't be using a shovel." He wadded up the paper the hamburger had been wrapped in and threw it at the trash can.

Ivy stood up and took his hand. Then he drove her home.

If you have enjoyed this book and would like to receive details of other Walker mystery titles, please write to:

Mystery Editor
Walker and Company
720 Fifth Avenue
New York, NY 10019